Never Say Never

The Never Knights #1

kailin gow

Never Say Never (The Never Knights Series)

A NOTE FROM THE AUTHOR

Thank you for choosing Never Say Never. I wanted to write about a young woman who was the lead and manager of a rock band full of young men and what it was like to be a woman in a tough industry. Along the way, I also wanted to write a different coming of age story, of a young woman finding out what she wanted.

College is all about learning and discovering, as well as finding out who you are and what you want to do, and perhaps whom you want to do it with.

For many, it is also the time to become independent. For me, that was the case.

I worked as a DJ, radio host of a women's show, and as a student peer adviser at the women's center on campus when I was an undergraduate. And I would come across incidences of regrets and issues from many women who felt pressured to do what they truly didn't want.

If you can relate to this book and to Never, know that your body is yours no matter how you dress, no matter if you're a private person or constantly in the public eye, no matter if you are already in a sexual relationship with someone. Your body is yours, and you have the right to feel secure in it. And no one has the right to make you feel inferior.

If you ever come across sexual harassment, stalking, bullying or anything that makes you feel unsafe, please seek help, speak up, and tell others. There are help centers everywhere on campus and in the community.

Speaking out is empowerment. Your body is yours.

Never Say Never (The Never Knights Series)

This is a YA-Mature/New Adult novel which may contain scenes not suitable for younger teens. Recommended age of reading is 17 years and up.

Kailin Gow

Never Say Never
Published by THE EDGE
THE EDGE is an imprint of Sparklesoup Inc.
Copyright © 2012 Kailin Gow

For information, please contact:

THE EDGE at Sparklesoup
14252 Culver Dr., A732
Irvine, CA 92604
www.sparklesoup.com
First Edition.
Printed in the United States of America.

ISBN: 978-1-59748-016-1

DEDICATION

For anyone who dares to dream.

Kailin Gow

Prologue

I feel the sweat pouring down my body. The feedback from the amplifier reverberates in my ears; my body is shaking to the sound of Geoff's guitar. The music is pulsing; I can feel it all around me in waves, feel my body twisting and turning as my voice echoes through the microphone, refracting like shattered glass through the room. I feel the energy of the keyboards – their sound like an electric shock thrilling my whole body with every movement. I feel the slow throbbing beat of the drums deep within my belly and I sing harder, sing louder, to catch the glory before it fades. They're all dancing – their eyes closed, locked in a trance, swaying together, cheering us on. Beautiful people – girls who look like models and men with eyeliner and leather jackets – the kind of defiant half-punk ecstasy you only get in nightclubs like these. Steve had been worried they wouldn't accept us. "The clientele at Veridium's the hardest crowd in the biz," he'd said. But I'd known as soon as we started playing that they'd love us. I knew it from the look in their eyes – that look of surprise, of shock, of vague recognitions that we were playing something great, and we were playing on the strings of their souls. The second the music had started up I'd felt the crowd shift – flint-eyed models accustomed to looks of disdain closing their eyes and waving their arms in the air, for one brief and glorious second not worrying about the poses they were making or whether or not happiness had calories. Trendy cocktail-makers behind the bar spilling their drinks as the whole zinc bar reverberated with our sound. *We had them.* I could feel our effect; I could feel the effect the audience had on me: they were offering us their love, their admiration, their adoration.

Just like paradise, I thought. Because that's what this was – paradise. They say Los Angeles is the city of Angels. Well, tonight I was an angel – an angel in a punk-rock tank and a beat-up leather skirt and spiky boots that came up to my thighs – and tonight I was in heaven. I'd always known this is what I wanted to do – to sing strange songs at three in the morning in an LA nightclub, to make girls' mascara drip down their faces when they cried while singing along, to feel this energy flooding through me like an electrical storm.

I'd never had the voice for opera. I'd learned that

long ago, when Dad had reluctantly caved into my relentless pressure to hiring a vocal tutor for me. My voice wasn't clean and pure and formal, that's what the tutor had said. It was raw – animalistic – powerful without ever being controlled. It wasn't a voice to lace up into corsets or pretty costumes; it wasn't the voice to hum along to on the radio. It was husky – sweet only when I tried – filled with emotion and rage and somewhere in there I could carry a tune. The classically trained soprano my dad had hired had thrown up her hands when I refused to moderate my tones for the fiftieth time and said, "Well, I don't know how she does it – but she's got a voice like her father, all right."

Some girls have their fathers sing them lullabies. My dad sang me punk rock from the time I was six months old. The one time he sang me "Hush Little Baby" backstage at a rock concert, one of the groupies recorded it on camera and it hit the celebrity gossip shows in a matter of hours; today, you can buy the bootleg "Lullaby EP" on the Internet if you know where to look. I didn't grow up with too much "Baa Baa Black Sheep," anyhow – my father used to sing me his greatest hits instead. "Black Death," "Eyes of Defeat," "Your Endless Hurt." He used to sing in that raw, wild voice of his and caress me with his guitar-calloused hands and I grew up singing all of his greatest hits in the shower.

Of course, I didn't know he was Keith Knight – *the* Keith Knight. The guy who'd shown up to the Grammy Awards in blue eyeliner and a black leather doublet with a parakeet on his shoulder. The guy David Bowie had once said he wished he could have been. By the time he had me, all traces of the drug-addled, androgynous, heavily made-up, leather-clad glam rock star my mother had fallen in love with had fallen by the wayside. The Keith Knight I knew was a family man – he'd gone off drugs the second he'd heard my mom was pregnant – slightly pot-bellied, with nothing to suggest to me that he was anything but a normal dad except for the characteristic twinkle in his eye. To his fans, of course, my dad was still Keith Knight of the Dark Knights, the eighties punk-glam band that defined a generation. But to me, he was just Dad.

My eyes quickly scanned the crowd for familiar faces. I could make out a few amid the sea of anonymity. A place like Beverly Hills is a small town – if you know it well enough. The same kinds of people go to all the same parties. Minor celebrities, a couple of socialites, a potential reality TV show star in the making trying to talk her way past the bouncers at the door. A few cynical-looking older men who assume that the only reason I'm here at all, the only reason the Never Knights are even playing, is because of my father and his credentials.

Please. If my dad knew I was out here, I'd be grounded. Not that I could be grounded anymore, of course – at 18, I was a freshman at USC and out of the house for the first time and leading one of the hottest up-and-coming bands in the music world.

Chapter 1

As we were packing up our instruments, I could feel the last of the adrenaline start to wear off. My face was flushed; my long dark hair was tangled with sweat and exertion. My makeup had run down my eyes, giving me the mild appearance of a raccoon. But I felt beautiful. I could feel my happiness and excitement emanating from every pore in my face, from every cell in my body. I walked over to the boys who were packing up their kit. "Hey guys!" I wrapped them all in a big bear hug. "You did an amazing job out there tonight. Couldn't you feel it? And if I'm not mistaken, I thought that I saw Richard Slayton in the crowd..."

This was enough to knock them into silence. They looked up at me in shock. "Really?" asked Kyle in a small voice. Then he broke out into a broad grin and laughed with joy and relief. Luc jumped up to his feet and gave me a high five, his skin hot against mine. "I told you to have faith," he said, "I knew he'd show. He wasn't going to miss this for the world. Not the Never Knights..."

Steve got up from his drum set, stretching his long and lanky frame. "Don't jinx it!" he said. "You know the rules. We're going to play it cool, Luc. Not going to get excited until it's in writing on the dotted line. I don't care if it's Richard Slayton or any other record exec – I don't want to jinx it. Besides..." his eyes trailed across the room to a pair of blonde twins giggling over at the bar. "I've got other things to worry about tonight. Those two were giving me the eye all evening. I don't want to be distracted." He laughed loudly. "If you know what I mean."

I rolled my eyes. Steve might be the world's biggest lady-killer now, but I remembered the awkward gangly kid he used to be, and the idea of him bagging not one, but two of those perfect-ten blondes in the corner was less awe-inspiring to me than faintly ridiculous. He was unmistakably handsome now, of course – if I was being rational I'd point out his emerald green eyes and affable, boyish charm – but somehow I couldn't get past seeing him as the muddy-faced pre-adolescent I used to mercilessly mock in the schoolyard.

"Color me impressed, Steve," I said loudly, trying to

match his masculine bravado word for word. "I remember when the ladies didn't even give you a chance to disappoint them. Just because you've managed to bulk up on egg-yolk-powder and protein shakes doesn't change anything – I know the truth. You're still the skinny-bones I remember."

Steve grinned widely, evidently ready for a challenge. "Freckle-face," he chanted back at me. "Don't get so high and mighty. I seem to remember you were a late bloomer."

"At least I didn't have a butt like a flat board," I laughed.

"At least I didn't have a flat *chest!*" Steve retorted, and the other boys laughed and whooped. They were used to our little teasing matches, and although I usually won, the boys liked to cheer on Steve as the underdog.

"Snot-nose."

"Pimply."

We were in each other's faces, now – barely an inch of space between us. As I looked into Steve's green eyes, watching them go vaguely cross-eyed at the lack of distance between us, we both gave up at the same time, collapsing into giggles and guffaws as the memory of our schoolyard banter came back to us. "Aw, come on, Neve,"

Steve put a muscular sweaty arm around me. He smelled of beer and guitar wood – a warm, reassuring smell I associated with our nights of jamming in Luc's basement.

"Aw, I'm just kidding, Neve. Those pimples cleared up good after a visit to the doctor. And let me tell you, I'm pretty sure you're not flat-chested, either. They can measure that these days – with science!"

"And I can't remember the days before you pumped all those steroids and developed those biceps," I replied sweetly. We laughed and hugged, and I grabbed Luc and pulled him into our group embrace. "Come on, guys, I heard they did a spread for us backstage. I don't know about you, but I'm starving." I was always starving after a shot – the expenditure of energy worked up a pretty intense appetite.

"Let's clean up later," Geoff assented. "Come on, I'm hungry too. And thirsty. Let's seize the moment."

We followed one of the staff workers into the back room, where we gasped at what we saw. There in front of us was an enormous table covered in black velvet cloth, piled high with buckets filled with ice – champagne and vodka bottles floating in them – and a mouth-watering spread of food: olives, pates, oysters, and several tiers' worth of delicious-looking chocolates. Everything was as elegant as I'd have expected it to be. Then again, Veridium was the kind of club that made its name on being elegant.

"Courtesy of Mr. Maxwell Simmons," the club manager said, smiling broadly. "He wants you to have the best amenities while you're here – as a thank you for such a good show. And he hopes you'll make a habit of coming back here."

"Tell him thank you for us," I smiled widely. "We really appreciate it – me and the guys. We all do."

"I'll let him know," the manager vanished through a mahogany door. For a moment as I looked at the food, I felt almost guilty. I'd been used to the royal treatment my whole life. I'd never been carded at a single club, no matter how exclusive or expensive – certainly, nobody here cared that any of us was under twenty-one. I'd been offered freebies like this my whole life – it was one of the perks of being Keith Knight's daughter. Everyone wanted my picture taken in one of their clubs, next to one of their friends. But as I looked over at the others, I felt embarrassed, turning pink. While Steve's family was relatively wealthy, neither Luc – whose dad was a police officer and whose mother was a teacher – nor Kyle, who'd been raised by his aunt, my dad's housekeeper, after his dad got sent to jail, had anything like the upbringing I'd had. It was one of those things I tried to forget about – one of the few things that separated us. But when we got treatment like this...

"How did you score this one?" Geoff looked at me, grinning widely. I couldn't help but feel annoyed – he'd found my insecurity and picked up on it.

"Actually," Luc broke in. "It was me this time."

I turned to Luc in surprise. "Oh?" I felt relieved.

"Max Simmons' daughter Cinna really likes our music. She's a big big fan – if you know what I mean."

"She's a big big fan of *yours,* you mean?"

Luc blushed. "That's exactly what I mean." He looked through the door and pointed her out, but he didn't need to. Six foot two and wearing designer minis that cost more than several bottles of the finest champagne, Cinna Simmons was every inch the stereotype of the LA socialite. She wasn't just beautiful – she was *expensive* – every part of her molded into perfection by the best tailors and surgeons money could buy. She caught sight of Luc through the door and waved, her perfectly-aligned cheekbones turning pink with pleasure. Steve had already wandered off, and had his arms around the two blondes.

Luc went over to Cinna, who embraced him with more-than-platonic intensity, and I watched as Kyle quickly became submerged in another crowd of female fans.

"Looks like everyone's partnering up," I said to Geoff as Kyle vanished.

"Yeah, guess so." Geoff took a step closer to me. "Which incidentally leaves us just where I want us to be, alone."

He lightly placed his fingers on my arm, moving them up to my shoulders.

Annoyance coursed through me. If there had ever been anything romantic between me and any of the band mates, it had long been repressed on all our sides out of the interest of our continuing friendship. We knew exactly how many bands had broken up because of personal infighting – and we didn't want that to be us. Only Geoff didn't listen. In the past few years, it seemed, he'd gotten it into his head that he was irresistible – that no woman could ever refuse him. And somehow this made me the ultimate prize. I was off-limits.

I gently removed his fingers and stepped back, making my stance clear. "Geoff, I don't want to have to tell you again. I'm not into that and you know it. I can't date you, Geoff. I can't date *anyone* from the band."

"Guess I just have to quit, then..." Geoff sighed heavily. "Then would you break your rule?"

"I remember when the band was your life," I couldn't help snapping. "You wouldn't even have thought about quitting then."

"I guess you're just special then, Neve."

To my immense relief, Kyle reappeared with a chilled bottled soda for me. "Trying it on again, are we, Geoffrey? I'm warning you, Geoff – charm doesn't get far with Neve." He handed me the bottle and we clinked bottles. "Isn't that right Neve?"

"Absolutely," I said. "Like he said, Geoff. Charm won't get you an inch."

"Miss Knight?" A male voice interrupted our conversation.

I turned around and my mouth dropped open. Before me stood Dick Slayton – the most powerful producer in the record industry. And he had just addressed me by name.

We all fell silent, an expectant pause washing over us.

"Yes?"

"I enjoyed watching you perform tonight," he said and my stomach began to tense up with terror. "Your band has a lot of promise."

He motioned for me to follow him, and we went over to a private corner of the room. "I'm glad you think so..." I started. "How *much* promise, exactly?"

"Miss Knight, I'll be truthful here. You've got talent – raw, primal, animal talent. But what you need to work on is technique. That energy you had tonight – it's great. But you can never guarantee a thing like that. When a room works – it's magic. But when it doesn't – you need to make sure you have solid technique, solid practice under your belt to keep things going. Before RRR can consider you, we'd like to see a few more performances under your belt, a bit more polish in your sound."

"Oh..." My face fell and my stomach dropped.

"But in a few months' time, Miss Knight, I think you should drop us another invitation. I'd be most interested in seeing where you go from here, and I get the feeling that if you improve as much in the next few months as you've done in the last few, we might have room for you at our label."

"So this isn't a yes or a no?"

"There are no guarantees in life, Miss Knight. If you want an answer, we'll need to see more. I certainly look forward to seeing where and how you develop a few months down the line."

I wasn't sure whether to feel ecstatic or crushed. On the one hand – this wasn't a firm "yes," far from it. Mr. Slayton didn't think we had what it took just yet.

On the other hand, "in just a few months..." My heart began to beat faster and faster. Could we really have the potential to make it big?

"We'll definitely get a few more performances in, sir," I said, nervously shaking Mr. Slayton's hand.

"Glad to hear it, Miss Knight," said Mr. Slayton, bowing his head ever so slightly in a farewell as he walked off.

I returned to Kyle, who was sitting alone – Geoff having gone to try on his charming-rocker act with a few girls more into it than I was. I shook my head. When we were kids Geoff had been great – respectful, smart, passionate about the band. But lately, it seemed that all he cared about was getting girls and doing drugs. His performance in the band was slipping – we all knew that, but none of us wanted to admit it. He had talent, but he practiced less than any of us.

"What did he say?" Kyle turned to me with his enormous blue eyes.

I told Kyle what Mr. Slayton had said.

"Hmm," Kyle considered, putting his arm around me. "Well, don't worry, Neve. We'll get there in the end – even if it means practicing every day for the next six months. Have we ever let you down yet?"

"No," I admitted, smiling slightly. "You haven't. We'll get there. I know it."

Kyle looked deep into my eyes, and I could feel the warmth – the trust – in his gaze. "I have every faith in you. In us," Kyle said gently.

"Thanks." I rested my head against Kyle's chest as he gently pulled me towards him. There was something so reassuring about his touch. I'd gotten a lot of teasing about my relationship to the four so-called hotties of The Never Knights from the girls at USC, but I knew they were wrong. What I had with Kyle – what I had with all the boys, since we were kids, except maybe Geoff – went beyond attraction, beyond sex. We were like family: a relationship more important than mere romance.

"We're going to do it our way," I said. I knew the

alternative – capitalize on my dad's name, get a reality TV show and a record deal in ten seconds flat if I was willing to throw up at a nightclub or get into a catfight or have sex on camera and leak it to the press. All I needed was a camcorder and a willing partner and I'd be top of the tabloids in no time.

But I didn't just want fame. None of us did. We wanted something bigger. We wanted to change the world with our music, with our art.

"I know he makes it hard for you," said Kyle, and I knew immediately he was talking about my dad. "But if you *do* make it – you'll do it the way he did. As hard-headed and stubborn as he is." He coughed slightly and flushed red. "Speaking of your dad, my aunt says your parents are expecting you home this weekend."

He always got a bit embarrassed. I loved Mrs. Jostens, his mother's sister and my dad's long-suffering housekeeper, but neither one of us liked to acknowledge that he'd grown up as the live-in nephew of my dad's live-in maid.

I groaned and rolled my eyes, trying to steer the conversation into a topic we could both relate to.

"I was looking forward to a night out in the dorms.

I've only been in college for two weeks!"

"I know, right?" Kyle laughed. "Then again, when I tried to use the washer in the dorm laundry room it got jammed – apparently someone left about twenty condoms in there as a joke and they clogged up the whole machine. I wouldn't mind some home-cooked food and an ironing board."

Kyle shot me his signature angelic smile.

"You can take me home," I said. "You haven't been drinking, have you?"

"I had a couple of sips of beer an hour ago – but I'm definitely under the limit. Unlike Geoff."

"I don't want *him* taking me home!" I announced hotly.

"Was he being creepy again?"

I rolled my eyes. "It's not cool. I've said 'no,' I mean 'no,' and that's that. I didn't want him before, and I want him even *less* now that I know apparently he doesn't take "no" for an answer. What girl wants to be brow-beaten into having sex with him?"

"You want me to have a word with him?" Kyle said.

"No," I said. "*I* want to have a word with him. When he's sober enough to remember what I said the next morning. If he cops a feel one more time while 'checking the mic' I'm going to hit him with his own guitar..."

We were interrupted by the sound of crashing glass from the other room, followed by a male moan of pain and a girl's shriek.

"I didn't do anything!" she was screaming.

We rushed into the other room to find Geoff in the middle of a shattered glass table, wincing in agony. His arm was covered in blood.

"He wouldn't leave me alone..." the girl's voice faltered. "I finally pushed him away – he sort of staggered over and fell into the table..."

"Oh, for fuck's safe, Geoff..." I went over to him. "What have you done...?"

"Ouch..." The alcohol had evidently numbed Geoff to the severity of the pain. Shards of glass were sticking out of his arm; it was painful just to look at him.

"Call 9-1-1," I said, my voice automatically reverting into "responsible mode." "Responsible mode" was one of those things my dad had been careful to teach me early on – he'd watched one of his first band mates die from choking on his own vomit after a night of drinking, unable to save him, and it wasn't an experience he wanted me to repeat. "We need to get him to the hospital, now!"

"Already called," Luc walked over.

"Geoff – you're gonna be fine, but you've got to stay still, okay...?"

"I think I broke my arm..." Geoff was murmuring. "How am I going to play guitar now?"

Luc and I looked at each other. Geoff was right. Looking at his injuries, I could tell he'd be out of commission for a while.

"You're fine, Geoff; you'll be fine. Just wait for the paramedics to come help you, okay?"

But I knew with a sinking feeling that we'd need to hunt for a new guitarist....

Chapter 2

It was good to be home again. As much as I hated to admit it, living in a Beverly Hills mansion with thirteen bedrooms and a swimming pool *was* a lot nicer than sharing a filthy USC dorm room with a girl who had a habit of vomiting in the wastepaper basket after a night out and covering up her nightly cigarettes with sickeningly sweet patchouli incense. Plus, Kyle was right – Mrs. Jostens was a lot better at doing laundry than I was; I'd already managed to turn my white dress a pale shade of dirty pink.

But I didn't want to admit it. I'd told my dad I wanted to be independent, and I meant it. I resolved to ask Mrs. Jostens to teach me how to iron my clothes properly without my dad finding out – he'd just mock me in that good-natured way of his.

It's just two weeks into freshman year, I told myself. *You're not meant to figure all this stuff out right away.* Still, the ruined pink dress was like a badge of shame. *You might think you're self-sufficient, Neve Knight, but you're still a spoiled baby at heart.*

Never mind, I told myself. I'd learn. I headed down to the laundry room, finding Kyle sitting at the kitchen counter, wolfing down an enormous fried breakfast of bacon, eggs and sausages.

"Careful there, fatty," I said, stealing a slice of bacon off his plate. "You won't be able to fit through the door soon."

Kyle laughed and rolled his eyes. If there was anything Kyle wasn't, it was fat. He was as lean and fit as a fitness model – his metabolism converting every calorie of bacon into firm, taut muscle. He'd even done a few modeling shoots to pay for college – my mother had managed to talk her agent into giving him a shot in the latest swimsuit edition – and with his preppy blond hair, hard abs, and sleek golden boy looks, I figured I'd see him on the cover of *GQ* sooner or later.

I sat down next to him, and he scooped some of his breakfast onto my plate.

"Better than dorm swill, huh?" I said. "Your aunt's got to be the best cook on the planet."

"Amen..." Kyle pushed a glass of orange juice

towards me.

"Maybe we should get some Tupperware," I said, "bring her food back with us to the dorms."

"Let's not," Kyle said. "Or your fat-jokes will turn into a reality before you know it. I can't eat like this every day or my agent will put me on one of those juice fasts."

"To be fair – if it's a juice fast or dorm food, I'd pick the fast." I laughed. "Careful, though. If you want to compete with Steve as the most ripped guy in the band, you'll have your work cut out for you!"

We both burst out laughing. Steve's overnight metamorphosis from scrawny stick-figure, the victim of several bully attempts in middle school, to bulked-up athlete had taken us all by surprise.

"Oh, please," said Kyle. "Everyone knows Steve gets up at six to "work out." "Delayed puberty" my ass – that guy *works* for his body. Me, I'm too lazy. Once I turn forty or fifty and my metabolism slows down, I'll look like Santa Claus. And you know what? By then I won't mind. I'll be a famous rock star and nobody will be able to say anything."

"Come on!" I said. "Unfortunately, I can't say the same." I'd grown up around the tabloids – and I knew exactly how cruel they could be to women who didn't fit the mold. My mother, Jessica Botano – a former swimsuit model – had gained a bit of weight when I was around twelve – barely noticeable to me, of course – and the tabloids had savaged her for weeks with vicious puns and photos taken of her in our pool. Not that anyone – tabloid or otherwise – had dared to criticize my father's paunch.

I had secretly resolved to, when I was as famous as my dad, dump the diet – eat as much as I wanted – and give the proverbial finger to any tabloid that dared to criticize me for it. Unfortunately, to get there, as much as I hated it, I had to play the looks game for a while.

"When we're forty we can stop working out," I said. "Unfortunately, we're not forty yet. Let's head to the gym, okay?"

Working out was always much more fun with Kyle present. Normally I got bored on the machines, but with Kyle we could take turns on the boxing bag, gossiping about whom we wished the bag was this week, taking out our aggressions. When I performed, I wore stage makeup – I think there's a law in LA about going out without at least a bottle of mascara on each eye – but only Kyle and Steve had seen me in my natural state: a sweaty, red-cheeked, barely out-of-pimpliness mess. They didn't seem to mind.

"So, whom should we punch this week?" Kyle grinned his cheeky grin as he wiped off the sweat with a towel.

"Geoff," I said without missing a beat. "Between his womanizing and his stupidity in the bar last Friday...I don't know what I'm more annoyed about, that he got himself injured or that he was dumb enough to make a woman push him away in the first place." I sighed, giving the bag a solid punch. "I feel bad for him and all – but he's really been unreliable lately. Slayton says we need more performances if we want to get signed – and our booker's got a ton of gigs lined up for us. None of which we can play without a lead guitarist."

"How long do you think Geoff will be out of commission?" Kyle asked.

"Long enough," I rolled my eyes. "He had a piece of glass sticking out of his arm – it was disgusting! I doubt he's going to be picking up a guitar anytime soon."

"Then who's going to play lead?" Kyle sighed. "Can't you..."

"I'm nowhere near good enough. I can hold a melody on the guitar in a pinch but I've got fingers like sausages when it comes to the solos. You know that."

"Then who...?"

"Beats me."

"We'll have to ask around."

"Geoff may be a sleaze, but he's a sleaze who can *play.*"

"We could ask if your dad knows..."

"No!" I said.

"Don't stress." Kyle put up his hands in mock self-defense. "We'll find someone. It'll be okay."

"If only we all had your sunny attitude, Kyle." I smiled reluctantly at his inveterate cheeriness. Kyle knew just how to keep me confident.

"Got it from you, Neve." He smiled shyly. "Family resemblance?" He laughed. "You're basically family, after all. I can't remember a time before I lived here."

Can't, I couldn't help wondering, or *don't want to?* Kyle didn't talk much about the time before he'd come to live with his aunt, when he was six. But my dad had told me what had happened. His dad – a drunk who liked to rough him up – had shot his mother in front of him, and had gotten life in jail. His mom got a funeral that wasn't covered by her life insurance. Mrs. Jostens – and us – were all that he had in the world.

"I can't either," I said, slipping my hand in his. "What would I do without you around to boost my ego when I'm down?"

"I'm just flattering you to get into your pants, clearly!" Kyle laughed. It was a joke we'd made a hundred times before – the sort of fake flirting that felt safe precisely because we knew it would never go anywhere. Normally I'd have just laughed it off. But somehow we both fell into an awkward, strange silence. He hadn't meant it – at least, he hadn't *meant* to mean it. But for the first time, the joke didn't seem so funny.

I forced myself to laugh. "Don't you pull a Geoff on me, Kyle. Or I'll have to put *you* through a glass table and then where would we be?"

He seemed relieved by the laughter, and started laughing too. "Please, I wouldn't even *have* to flatter you. According to the girls at USC, I'm apparently fresh meat – I've never had so many girls interested in me at once! Or *ever.* You'd be *lucky* to get with me, Neve!"

"Sure I would," I said, forcing the joke. "I've just been pining for you my whole life. Wishing you'd notice me..."

"I thought you were like Queen Elizabeth,"

"What?"

"You know. The Virgin Queen of England. Refused to ever get married so she could focus on ruling her country."

"It's not that I'm not interested in dating," I said. "I'd just never date anyone in the band...I've seen the VH1 specials. I know that's the surest way to break up the group."

"So why not date someone outside the band?"

"I don't *know* anyone outside the band!" It was true. My band – Kyle, Luc, Steve, and even Geoff, no matter how much he annoyed me lately – were the only friends I was really close to. We spent all our time together; I didn't have a second free to date anyone I might see as a potential.

"Well, don't feel sorry for me," said Kyle. "Because I'm doing just fine outside the band." He seemed a little on edge – almost defensive. I looked up at him in surprise. Was there something *there* between us? I laughed it off. I used to dress Kyle in my life-size Barbie clothes when I was seven – I'd definitely seen him naked a couple of times when we were changing our swimming clothes. We knew each other too well to feel sexual tension.

Then why did things feel so weird all of a sudden?

"Neve?" A female voice interrupted our conversation, followed by the appearance of my mother – which, as it had done consistently for the past ten years, made Kyle's jaw drop. Whatever feelings Kyle might have for me – feelings I refused to acknowledge, they paled beside his long-standing crush on my mother. In her early forties, my mother managed to look barely older than I was. I knew a lot of former models resorted to plastic surgery and punishing pilates to look gorgeous, disguising their age, but none had maintained quite the youthful vitality of my mother.

"I missed you!" My mother ran to embrace me. "Two weeks was too long! Are you *sure* you don't want to commute to and from class – I'm sure Paul could drive you there and back every day..."

"I don't need a chauffeur, mom," I smiled. "I need a tiny dorm full of messy clothes and empty pizza boxes. The real college experience. You know that."

"Can't you have the real college experience from the pool house? It's got its own kitchen, you know – you could put the pizza in your fridge..."

"I don't think that fits the definition of 'real adult'.

Living in mom and dad's pool house."

"A lot of girls here do...Barry Monroe's daughter..." Dad's former band mate lived just down the road.

"Barry Monroe's daughter never goes to class and has her dad call up her professor and exchange autographs for A's. I don't want that."

My mother sighed. "But we worked *hard*," she said. "So you wouldn't have to."

I flushed red. I loved my mother, but she could be a bit oblivious sometimes – and right now, talking about money in front of Kyle, whose aunt probably worked a lot harder (although, to be honest, Kyle was too busy staring at my mom's stunning swimsuit curves than listening to the words coming out of her mouth), she was being especially oblivious. She'd been discovered at sixteen in a shopping mall in Texas, catapulted to the top of her field in a matter of months – like my dad, she'd never really known what it was like to live without the easy world of fame and money. And as much as I loved her, I knew that that sort of a life wasn't for me. I wanted to find my own way as much as possible.

"I want to work hard," I said. "I want to *learn* stuff – I've got this great History of Classical Music class at 8 a.m. I'd *never* make it to if I had to drive from here...I want to earn my grades. I don't want to just be the daughter of Keith Knight and Jessica Botano."

"I guess," my mother looked unconvinced. "I just want you to be safe out there, you know." She finally noticed Kyle. "Well, if Kyle's with you, I'll feel more confident that you're safe."

"I'll keep an eye on her, ma'am," said Kyle, only stuttering slightly.

"Most students grew up without a private security detail," I said, "and they do okay."

"But most students don't have paparazzi who can capture them in a moment of indiscretion..." my mother sighed.

"I'll keep the paps away," said Kyle.

"Well, I feel better knowing Kyle's with you," my mother admitted. "He's at least sensible, as opposed to my stubborn, hot-headed little girl..."

"I prefer the term 'passionate'," I smiled.

Kyle did too. He knew I'd become a skilled pro at negotiating these waters with my parents.

"Anyway," my mother changed the subject airily. "Can't we turn up the A/C? It's like a furnace down here.

And Kyle – Stacey's been asking for you. The guy we booked for the Ralph Lauren shoot turned out to be a junior member of the Russian mob and now she's desperate for a replacement..."

"I'll call her," Kyle said. "Thanks, Mrs. Knight..." He tiptoed out, leaving me alone with my mother.

"Thank God you're back!" My mother embraced me. "The house is so *old* without you. Your dad just wants to stay in, pop in a few Turner Classic Movies, eat popcorn – I swear, you'd never believe this was the man who once bit the head off a..." She lost her train of thought. "Although you wouldn't believe what he's doing tonight!"

"What?"

"He's invited his old friends around...for a *sit down dinner*. The Dark Knights – sitting and eating with a fork and knife in a formal dining room – can you picture that?"

My mom was a groupie back in the day when my dad used to trash formal dining rooms with a vengeance. She found it harder than he did to let that go.

"Are they going to have a *cheese course?*" my mom laughed.

"Probably," I sighed.

"I know I said it would just be us," my mom put an

arm around me. "But would you mind hanging with those old fuddy-duddies for a while?"

I smiled. "Not at all."

.

Chapter 3

If my mother had been worried that my dad had gotten a bit too old for the rock and roll life, she certainly didn't need to be. No sooner had David, Leroy, and John arrived – a bit fatter than they had been, uniformly balding, their hair gray and tangled – than the four of them started behaving as if a time warp had brought them back to 1979. The classy white wine that Kyle had poured out for them at the beginning of the meal was replaced by significantly less classy beer after the second course, and halfway through dessert my father got raucously bored and decided to order thirty pizzas from the local shop, laughing as he slurred his words on the phone to the increasingly confused delivery boy.

"Yes, you got it. Thirty pepperoni pizzas for *the* Keith Knight. Exactly. And a vegetarian one for Leroy Milford. No, I'm not joking – Leroy Milford, the bassist, he's right here in my house..."

My father looked up in shock.

"He hung up on me. Told me to stop playing pranks. Didn't believe I was Keith Knight."

The band all branched into raucous laughter. I caught Kyle's eye, smiling at my mother's consternation. My father might be strict "dad" to me, but to his band mates he was still the cool, iconic rock star he had been twenty and thirty years before. Before long, they were standing on the table, belting out hits:

"Every time I look into your eyes/
I feel the beat of your dark..."

My father was shrieking, using the wine bottle as a microphone.

"Careful!" My mother narrowly avoided being decapitated by his cup. "Watch it, Keith, you're going to..."

John, the old keyboardist, turned to me. "So, you got any thoughts of going into the biz, girl?"

"She does not!" my father interrupted immediately. "She's going to go to law school and become a lawyer and be the only responsible one in our family."

"Actually..."

"No way I'm letting her anywhere near a recording studio. She plays for fun – that's all..." Even standing on a table in leather pants, my father managed to make the authoritative "dad voice" sound strict and imposing. I said nothing – but Kyle and I had to resist collapsing into giggles.

I helped him clear the table and we escaped into the kitchen, laughing.

"So this is what celebrity does behind closed doors," Kyle snickered. "I was afraid your dad was going to bite the cork off the wine bottle..."

"I can't decide if having Keith Knight as a dad makes it more or less embarrassing when you see him dancing on a table. Probably more."

"No – he's still got it," said Kyle. "At least, that's what all the fan mail says."

"You've read my dad's fan mail?"

"He pays me to open it for him and sort out the crazies...apparently a lot of girls think your dad is *fiiine.*" He started teasing me. "There was this one girl, she sent a picture of her boobs."

"Ew!"

"She had a very detailed list of exactly what she

wanted him to do to her." Kyle grinned wickedly. "Let me see if I can remember it. "I want you to take off all my clothes, spray whipped cream all over my..."

"That's my *dad* you're talking about!" I hit Kyle playfully.

"There was definitely some creative utilization of strawberries."

"I don't want to hear it," I joked.

"That'll be you one day with the creepy fan mail."

"I hope not. I'm allergic to strawberries. Besides, without Geoffrey, we're not even going to make it to the D-list."

Our concerns about finding a replacement guitarist were not alleviated by the end of the weekend. Sunday morning our booker called me to say she'd scored us a gig at Club House, the coolest coffee-house-cum-brewery on the whole West Coast. Overwhelmed by our good fortune, I neglected to mention to her that our lead guitarist had a broken arm and several bruised fingers – and the next night, when we all met for dinner at Luc's house to jam in his basement, my nerves were beginning to get frayed.

"We've only got five days!" I was saying to Steve as we tried – in vain – to help Luc's mama, Mrs. Alamo in the kitchen, before being shooed away with an Italian curse word or two. "How are we supposed to find a lead guitarist in five days?"

"We can hold auditions," Steve said. "Don't worry. I've already put out an ad on Craigslist and posted adverts in all the music shops between here and San Francisco."

"But who's going to be as good as Geoff?"

"We'll find someone – and someone who knows how to hold his liquor at that." Steve grinned. "Don't worry, Neve. You'll get full rights of refusal over anyone we find."

"He's got to be incredible – whoever we find. I mean, if Slayton's looking to see how much we improve, he'll send his scouts to our shows; the pressure's going to be intense. We can't afford to do anything but the best job – we have to absolutely blow his mind."

"I know," said Steve. "Believe me – we'll find something incredible."

"Enough worry!" Luc's mother interrupted, placing an enormous family-sized plate of spaghetti with tomato sauce on the table. "First pasta – then you can worry."

I couldn't think of a family more unlike my own than Luc's. Luc's mother – a tiny woman from Naples who taught Italian at the local public school – was as traditionally maternal as mine was unconventional: she was warm and vivacious and always concerned that I wasn't getting enough nutrition. "Too skinny!" she informed me. "Sophia Loren always said she got her amazing curves from spaghetti. You could be as beautiful as Sophia Loren – but you have to have a little more meat on your bones, eh?" She reserved equal amounts of worry for her two daughters, Jennifer and Amy, who were fifteen and fourteen, respectively. "Why are you not eating? You will look like a scarecrow!"

As it happened, Jennifer and Amy *did* look like scarecrows – not merely because they were terribly slender, puberty not having quite caught up with them yet, but more pertinently because they sat in absolutely petrified stillness. They quite evidently had crushes on Steve and Kyle – unsure of which they thought was cuter – and managed to get by in their presence through an awkward combination of flirtation and freezing up in terror whenever one of the boys asked them a question.

"Careful, Steve," I whispered. "Don't start breaking their hearts young, or I'll have to come after you myself."

"Please, they're *kids*!" Steve whispered back. "Although I could have sworn we had some girls their age in the club last week – I'm convinced they're letting them in with fake IDs. One girl barely looked old enough to watch a PG-13 movie."

Still, they managed to accept the girls' crushes with charm and grace, being friendly and warm without ever leading them on. When the meal was over, they both kindly offered to help the girls with washing the dishes, sending them both a shade of scarlet even darker than the tomatoes left on the plate.

Luc smiled and rolled his eyes. "Come on, Neve," he said. "Let's get out of here, sit in the garden. It's getting hot with all these people in here."

We walked out into his garden. It was a beautiful, balmy September night. I closed my eyes and inhaled the sweet scent of the magnolias blooming in his backyard. Luc sat down on a tire that swung from the old oak tree. "Remember this," he said, motioning for me to sit next to him.

"Yeah, of course I do. We used to swing on this all the time when we were kids." I sat down, and Luc laughed, springing to his feet and beginning to push me.

"You thought that if you swung high enough, you'd be able to jump off and land right on the moon."

"I remember that. I figured I just had to try a *little* bit harder."

"That's my Neve," Luc said, pressing his hands against my back as he pushed me harder still. "Always so driven. So ambitious."

The tire slowed to a stop and I couldn't help but smile at his words.

"See, there it is."

"There what is?"

"That smile. That smile that says 'everything's going to be fine.' That smile that makes me know everything's going to be okay, and that you're not going to worry."

"Worry?"

"You've had a frown on your face ever since you met with Slayton." He put a hand on my shoulder. "Listen, Neve – I know you care. We all do. But if RRR doesn't sign with us, it's not the end of the world. There are always other opportunities to knock. Other doors."

"But right now we have *this* opportunity," I couldn't help replying. "*This* door. He liked what he heard, Luc. He didn't say 'no.' And that means we could do it. We *can* do it. Or at least, we could, if it weren't for this thing with Geoffrey. But we've got what it takes, Luc. I can feel it. I'm sure of it."

Luc pressed his warm lips against my forehead. "I believe in you, Neve. I trust your instincts. If Slayton feels right to you, then let's go with that; I'll follow you, 110%."

I took his hand and squeezed it. "Thanks, Luc," I said. "That means a lot to me."

"Good." Luc held my hand against his cheek. "Because you know how much you mean to me. I don't like seeing you worried. I just want to see you happy."

I felt vaguely embarrassed at his kind words, and blushed in the moonlight. Usually Luc and I traded witty banter, not serious sentiment.

"You're so sweet," I said.

Yet as Luc leaned in, his chocolate-brown eyes grew dark, and I saw a pain there I had not seen before. "I'm not trying to be sweet, Neve," he said slowly, carefully. His whole face seemed transformed in the moonlight, and I could feel a strange shiver run up and down my body. He put one strong arm around my waist, sitting next to me as he pulled me into a tight hug. "I remember when we first met, Neve. We were just kids. I always figured you were the prettiest girl I'd ever seen. You still are, you know, but that's not all you are. You've got something else – something different. You're funny, fun to be around, and interesting, and smart – but more than that...you're *ambitious*. You have something I've never found in another girl – in another person..."

"What's that?"

"This...like this relentless drive in you. This passion that makes you always work so hard. And that's what makes me sure that you've got what it takes, Never. That you're going to make it. And I'm so excited – so lucky – to be a part of making that happen. To be a part of this."

As he spoke, I suddenly became aware of his lips mere inches from mine. A feeling – strange, indescribable, overwhelming – passed over me like a tidal wave, and I pulled back...

"Luc..." my voice was full of warning.

He stopped. He hesitated, as if making a decision. "Don't worry, Neve. I'm not trying to freak you out or pull a Geoff or anything. But...you're my friend, Neve. I care about you. We're friends, right?"

"Of course!"

"And...uh...I'd never do anything to get in the way of that. Or hurt you. You know that, right?"

"I know..."

But deep down, I felt that something had passed between us. My cheeks were bright red. "We should go back inside, Luc. Before your sisters make Kyle and Steve do all the dishes."

"Of course," said Luc, forcing a smile. The moonlight hit him as he walked and I involuntarily gasped. For a moment, I forgot that it was Luc standing before me – instead there was just a gorgeous man with dark Italian eyes and caramel-colored hair that made my heart involuntarily race.

I shook my head and tried to ignore it. What was going on with me today? First Kyle – then Luc? Was there something about going off to college that had sent all our collective hormones into a tizzy?

Come on, girl, I told myself. *The band comes first.*

But as I walked back into Luc's living room, I felt a strange sense of foreboding. Something had changed – something deep down within all of us. The more serious the band was getting, the closer we got to making it, the more we had to grow up. We all knew each other since middle school, but now we weren't prepubescent awkward kids anymore.

Things weren't going to be the same anymore.

Chapter 4

I'd decided to fulfill my necessary Sociology credit at USC by signing up for a Music-In-Society class – the somewhat transgressive-sounding "Starting a Riot: Music, Sexuality, and Gender in the Late Twentieth Century." I'd been somewhat embarrassed about signing up, despite my genuine interest in the topic – I was painfully conscious that it might look like I was striving for an easy A off my dad's stories – but I hadn't been able to resist the promise of studying my dad's punk lyrics alongside the poetry of the beat generation and the Stonewall riots. I tried to dress down for the class as much as possible – hiding my customary glam-inspired studs and black stiletto boots under an enormous USC sweatshirt in the hopes that nobody in the class would recognize me – at least not at first. The last thing I wanted was to be "Keith Knight's daughter" here in the classroom. I remembered what I'd said to my mother. I wanted to do this on my own – to forge my own path. And if that meant taking out my ear studs and cutting back on the purple mascara – well, I'd just have to sacrifice my glam aesthetic to the higher calling of knowledge. The class was taught by Professor Edmund Poe, an ethnomusicographer better known for his studies of Georgian polyphonic chant in the South Caucasus than for his experience in the punk music scene. But rumor had it that Professor Poe was going to be team-teaching the class with an English TA with some experience in the contemporary music industry.

"My dear ladies and gentlemen," Professor Poe stood up at the podium, standing on his tiptoes so that his bushy white hair could just barely be seen behind it. He couldn't have looked less like a rock star. With his wavy, tangled white hair, his enormous owlish glasses, and his stained tweed suit, he looked more like a professor of Medieval History than someone conversant with the lyrics of the Clash. "It gives me great pleasure to be standing in front of all of you as we prepare to embark upon this journey together. Music has long been a medium that brings individuals and societies together – it allows them to affirm their shared identity, or else – as we shall see in this semester's class – to subvert it entirely. Its power has been called spiritual – it has also been called dangerous. In the remote mountains of Svaneti, some tribes use music to hold onto a religious and cultural identity all but lost. On the streets of New York City and Los Angeles, some "tribes" used it to create their own identities. Perhaps some of you are wondering what an old fuddy-duddy like me has to say about Keith Knight or David Bowie..."

A few members of the class laughed along with his joke, but I flushed bright red. *Why did they always have to bring up my dad?*

"But this year I will be complementing my traditional ethnographic methods with what one might call a more *youthful* approach. As many of you know, it is customary within the department to teach alongside qualified teaching assistants – graduate students in our department who wish to gain experience of the classroom before seeking full-time teaching positions. Well, it is my great honor to introduce to you your TA and one of my very brightest research students, who is studying for a doctorate in the comparative imagery of gender in late nineteenth-century 'decadent' fiction and in the 'glam rock' of the 1970's. I would like to introduce you all to Danny Blue. Danny, would you stand up please?"

My mouth fell open. The tall young man in the

skin-tight black jeans and the black t-shirt couldn't have looked less like the typical graduate students. With his long jet-black hair that fell down to his shoulders, his piercing blue eyes, his chiseled Roman nose, high cheekbones, Danny Blue looked more like a rock star than a music scholar. As he sauntered up to the podium, his long ebony hair shining under the fluorescent lights of the classroom, I felt my heart skip a beat. He radiated sex appeal – the kind of raw animal magnetism that my father had always just called "it." That thing that rock stars either had – or never would have. That thing that separated the wannabes from the truly greats. And Danny Blue, sporting a leather jacket and what looked like the tiniest hint of eyeliner on his gorgeous, sky-colored eyes, had *it*.

I felt my face flush hot and red, embarrassment making the color brighter still. What was happening to me? I'd managed to pass my teen years without even the slightest hint of a crush on anybody – utterly uninterested in sex or romance. I'd had my hands full with work and the band – and between my dad's stories of groupies "back in the day" and the greasy wannabes in the club scene who used to hit on me just because I was Keith Knight's daughter and could probably get them a record deal, I'd basically been turned off to the idea of romance altogether. But somehow sitting in a desk in front of Danny Blue made me really regret wearing this sweaty USC shirt – a regret and self-consciousness utterly unlike anything I'd ever felt before.

"Thank you so much for that very kind introduction, Professor."

And that accent! Clipped, clear, and with just a slightest hint of Northern vowels, Danny Blue's English accent sent shivers up and down my body. "I daresay he's over-sold me quite a bit – he clearly hasn't read the latest draft chapter of my doctorate."

The class tittered, but I could sense that at least half the class was too busy checking out his rock-hard abs and muscular arms to care much about what he had to say. Even I – struggling to pay attention to what he said about the development of post-punk as a genre – couldn't help undressing him with my eyes, imagining what he might be wearing – or not wearing – underneath that tight black muscle-tee. There was something more than beautiful about him – there was a strange haunting sense of tragedy in his eyes – a brooding, mournful look that suggested that there was more to this Danny Blue than met the eye.

Is he looking at me? I felt my face grow hotter still as Danny Blue's icy eyes fixed upon me. *Why is he looking at me? Stop blushing, Neve...*

My mother always used to tell me the story of the first time she met my dad, screaming her head off at one of his concerts, catching his eye from across a crowded room. Was this how she felt?

It was almost a relief when class ended, and I could get away. I briefly switched on my phone, noticing a text from Steve.

Steve: *Ten for auditions. Got some recs. Meet at the apt. S.*

Luc and Steve – already sophomores at USC – shared an off-campus apartment near the dorms.

Me: *Will be there.*

I texted back, noticing Danny out of the corner of my eye. He was checking his phone, too, his expression tense with concentration. He looked up at me, noticing that we were doing the same thing, and smiled, sending my attempts at cool aloofness torpedoing into destruction. He slid his phone down the front pocket of his jeans and walked over to me as I stood up with my book bag. He was a full head and a half taller than I was, I noted – a feat; I was nearly five-ten myself, having inherited my mother's height and pretty much her build.

"I've got to ask," he said – his accent even more swoon-inducing than it had been a moment ago. "Have we met before? You look awfully familiar."

I turned even redder. If I told him that the reason I looked *awfully familiar* was because he'd probably seen my dad in concert, he'd probably think what the others did – that I was only taking this class like every other celebrity's daughter, for an easy A. "I just have one of those faces," I said, avoiding his gaze. "I get that a lot. I'm always being told I look like somebody...." *Neve, get a grip. Why are you stammering?* I never stammered. I never got this red or embarrassed around a guy, ever.

"I doubt that very much," said Danny. "You definitely don't have that kind of face. If I'd met you before, I'd remember, ah..."

"Neve," I said quickly.

"Neve what?" He looked down at his class list.

Damn it. "Neve Knight," I admitted. "It's – uh – it's

under Never Knight."

"Never Knight?" he smiled. "Like – Never Ever Never?"

"Exactly like that. But I just go by Neve."

"Were your parents hippies or something?"

I breathed a sigh of relief. He hadn't put two and two together yet.

"Yeah, you could say that."

"Pleased to meet you, Neve..." he said. Then he frowned, suddenly, his eyes darkening. *Does he know who I am?* "I imagine I'll talk to you more in the coming weeks. We'll be dividing up into small workshop seminars to work on our first-semester projects. We'll be choosing a decade and working on research presentations accordingly – so start thinking about which time period you want to work on, and we'll discuss music from then."

"Well if there's one thing I know about," I blurted out before I could stop myself, "it's music."

Idiot. I wanted to clap my hand over my mouth in shame. *Idiot.* Did I just tell Danny Blue, future doctorate in musicology, that I was a music expert?

But he didn't seem too offended. "Good," he chuckled softly. "Same here, really." He patted me lightly on the arm, sending electricity flying through my body. "Later, love," he said, striding off, and leaving me standing with my backpack, staring after him and gawking like a schoolgirl. I couldn't believe it. This guy had me grinning like an idiot in ten seconds flat.

Far from an easy A – this class was going to require every ounce of concentration to stop me from turning into a puddle of goo on the floor.

Chapter 5

That night I made an extra effort to change before the auditions, although I would never have admitted it to anyone but myself that it was because of Danny Blue. He'd caught me in sweats and a ponytail – well, this time, if he ran into me on campus, he'd see me in my glam rock glory. I squeezed into my favorite white skinny jeans, matching them perfectly to a pair of high-heeled silver sandals encrusted with spikes I'd cut off my dad's old jacket when I was ten. I had turned one of my dad's enormous T-shirts into a fashionable halter – the disparity in size was nothing scissors, a needle, and thread couldn't fix – fending off the night breeze with a black leather motorcycle jacket I'd picked up at a vintage store in San Francisco last summer. The perfect blend of glamour and grunge, I thought, intentionally smearing my eyeliner just a touch to give it that studied "morning after" look.

Not that I needed to dress up for Luc and Steve. Their apartment was the epitome of "dressed down" - filled with beanbag chairs, empty Chinese food containers, a games console or two, and a few piles of dirty laundry Luc had given up ever bringing to the bathroom and seemed to have converted into miniature cushions instead. *Typical guys,* I thought, smelling the familiar aroma of two-day-old pizza as I walked through the door.

"Looking good!" Steve laughed. "Did you get all dressed up for us, Neve? Or have you got a hot date tonight?"

"You know me," I said, trying not to think about Danny Blue's piercing eyes. "I've got two dates lined up, back to back." I settled down on the black leather sofa in the middle of the room, before catching sight of a lacy red bra sticking out between the cushions. "So, guys, is there – uh – something you want to tell me?" I threw the bra over to Steve. "Funny, I wouldn't have pegged Steve for a 32DD, myself. He looks more like a 36B to me."

Luc turned redder than the bra itself, his eyes downcast on the floor. Steve, however, only grinned.

"One of those blonde twins, was it?" I looked over at Steve.

"*One?*" Steve looked like a cat that had finished all the cream. "You underestimate me, my friend."

I rolled my eyes. "I don't even *want* to know." I picked up a pile of dirty socks. "Come on, guys. If we're going to hold auditions here tonight, can't we at least try to make the place look professional, okay?" I began moving the laundry into the bedrooms. "Come on guys – help a girl out?"

The others hurried to tidy up.

"So, who's coming tonight?" I asked.

Steve ran through the updated list. "We've got ten sign-ups so far," he said. "And two recommendations that some other bands sent us."

"We'll be up all night," Luc sighed. "If we want to get through all of them tonight."

"We don't have a choice," said Steve. "It's already Tuesday night. We need to decide tonight if we want to be ready by Friday. Even now it'll be a real stretch."

"So, okay," I thought for a while. "So if we give them each five minutes to play and about two to introduce themselves, we won't be more than an hour and a half, tops. That's not too bad. Then we can sit and deliberate."

"Hopefully we won't need to do call-backs." Steve smiled.

"Hopefully we'll get enough good people," I bit my

lip anxiously. Would anyone be as good as Geoff?

Our first option wasn't too promising. When we let "Farmer, John Farmer" through the door, he trudged in wearing a dirty white T-shirt that looked like it had never seen bleach in its lifetime and sneakers that had evidently been tracked through several fields' worth of mud. His shoelaces were untied and from the smell it seemed reasonably apparent that he hadn't showered for days.

Maybe he's just a Kurt Cobain type, I thought to myself, trying to force myself to be more optimistic than I felt.

"So, why do you want to play with us, man?" Steve was trying to be as friendly as possible, but "Farmer, John Farmer's," surly demeanor wasn't making it easy for him. Good old Steve, I thought. Always trying to be friendly – always trying to put the others at ease.

"I just think it's time for my big break," John said. "You know, I just need that one break-out gig so I can get famous, move into the big leagues – get my solo deal, you know?"

Luc and I exchanged looks. This guy was a textbook example of what we didn't want in a band member.

"I hope he's not good," Luc whispered into my ear. "Then we'd have to put up with him."

Luckily for us, he was utterly mediocre, and we felt no guilt when the door slammed behind him and we put a firm X next to his name on the audition list.

"Let's hope the others aren't all like him," said Kyle, "or else we're pretty screwed."

The next few were better – and among the mediocrity we picked out two or three players that we particularly liked – talented guitarists that could do more than hold a pick. A few even jammed with Steve and Kyle – and our spirits started to pick up. But the nagging feeling hadn't quite gone away. *None of these guys is as talented as Geoff – even if they are easier to work with...*

By the time the clock struck midnight, we'd all but decided on Eric Southey – a well-meaning USC senior with floppy surfer-blonde hair and a gravelly voice. We didn't feel amazing about him – he didn't quite have the "it" that Geoff managed to manifest when rocking out onstage on a Sunday night – but he was talented and solid and seemed like a hard worker.

And then the doorbell rang.

"My friend in The Taxi Cabs texted me this guy's

number," said Steve. "Said we had to give him a chance. I know it's last-minute, guys, but do you mind if we see one more?"

"Sure," Luc shrugged. "Neve, what do you think?"

I shrugged too. "Can't hurt."

But no sooner had our final candidate walked in through the door than I turned bright scarlet. There he was again, Danny Blue, looking sexier than ever in a black T-shirt that clung to his ripped, muscular body, leaving little of the chiseled contours of his painfully perfect abs to the imagination. He was wearing leather pants and black combat boots, his hair shining in the moonlight. I could feel myself trembling as I put down my head, hoping he wouldn't recognize me.

He still has to be good, Neve. We don't pick on looks – you know that. It's about the talent.

"Never Ever?" Danny Blue caught my eye. "I thought you looked familiar – why didn't you say you were from the Never Knights?"

My mouth opened involuntarily. So that's how he knew me.

"You know our work!"

"'Course I do. I caught your show at the Veridium

last week. Pretty solid, if I do say so myself. That's why I figured I'd come out here, see what you guys make of me. I'm sure you'll tell me I'm bollocks and send me home, of course. But I thought - what the hell, it's only an hour, I'll have a go, make a wanker of myself..." He laughed a charming, self-deprecating laugh, sweeping his long black hair out of his eyes. "I'd tell you all sorts of nice things about your voice, but you'd think I was just buttering you up to get into the band."

"I'm sure you're above such petty tactics," I said, unable to resist a smile at his easy charm.

"I'm sure *you've* heard all those nice things before. About your stage presence. About the way you sing like an angel and smile like a devil. All those things – sure you've heard them a million times! They won't affect you one bit."

And blush like a schoolgirl, I thought to myself bitterly. Still, if Danny Blue was trying to butter me up, he was doing a pretty good job.

"Aren't you going to try to flatter all of us?" Luc said, his smile ever so slightly twisted. "Suck up to all of us."

Danny laughed. "After," he said. "But first – I thought I might play you a little something. How about

'Rebel Rebel' – David Bowie? My favorite!"

"Mine too!" I couldn't resist blurting out.

And then he was playing, and all words died out like embers. From the moment his fingers first touched his guitar strings, I felt an energy buzzing through the room – an enormous, golden, pulsing force that seemed to enter each one of us in turn. All at once, it felt like we weren't in a smelly college apartment, weren't on some college campus – we were alone onstage just the two of us, me and him, feeling the rhythm of the music pulse through and overpower us. *This is it,* I thought to myself. *He's the one.* I had never been so sure of anything in my life.

Danny finished playing, the music still echoing on the amp as it faded into silence.

"I hope I didn't embarrass myself too badly," he said, a twinkle in his eye.

We were all silent. Then, we looked at one another – silently trading imperceptible nods.

"Welcome to the band," I said.

Chapter 6

We had no time to lose. It was already Tuesday night, and we had three full days to rehearse nonstop if we wanted to make a good impression for our Friday night gig. We were all running on adrenaline – we barely had time to introduce ourselves to each other before we stopped exchanging pleasantries altogether and started jamming. I had so many questions for Danny Blue – where had he learned to play the way he did? What was a doctoral student in ethnomusicography doing with a black leather trench coat that rivaled that of David Bowie? And what could account for that strange, sad, brooding look in his eyes? But I had no time to ask any of those questions. We didn't talk about anything that wasn't about pure business – frets, chords, tabs, and rhythm. I taught Danny the songs; Steve did a few licks on the drums. Everything was about music – just the way I liked it.

I was always the first person to complain when

personal talking infringed upon band time – I'd always been the first one to say "back to work." I didn't have a personal life; this band *was* my personal life. So why was I the one who, all of a sudden, felt a sting of disappointment when Danny said "back to work" and we didn't share more than two seconds of greeting before we were back to playing?

But the second Danny started on his guitar, I didn't want to do anything else. I never wanted to do anything else. His cracked, soft voice – at once harsh and sweet – the way he made the guitar strings quiver in his fingers and strain out beautiful music – his energy was something that washed over me like a tidal wave. My mind went blank; my thoughts were silenced. I no longer thought in words or phrases or lyrics – the pure *sound* of the melody was all that coursed through me like adrenaline or blood. That was the effect Danny Blue's music had on me. It made me crazy; it made me weak. But above all things it inspired me – made me feel that somewhere within our lyrics and our melodies and our jams there was some height of beauty that we had not reached, some summit we had not yet scaled or reached the peak of, and in Danny's piercing blue eyes I felt hope that we *would* get there. If only we practiced a little harder.

Unfortunately, by Wednesday night, we'd already experienced our first set-back. No sooner had we started a full run of our Friday night set list – crashed-learned between classes all day Wednesday – than there came a knock at the door. Luc sprang to his feet and opened the door to reveal Mr. Reynolds, the building superintendent, looking red and sheepish.

"I, uh, hate to bother you guys," he said. "But there have been a couple of complaints from the neighbors, you know. Apparently last night you guys were playing until pretty late..."

"Yeah, sorry about that," Steve said, blushing. *How could anybody object to Danny's playing?* I wondered.

"It's just – uh – you know the terms of the lease. Communal noise and all that. You guys can't really play after nine p.m., you know that. I've been pretty lax on you guys because you've been responsible, but once the neighbors start calling in it's off my hands."

"But we've got a gig on Friday!" Luc interrupted, his eyes wide with distress. "We're desperate – we need to practice..."

"Sorry guys," Mr. Reynolds ducked away. "Rules are rules, you know."

"Damn..." Kyle watched him go mournfully. "What could we do now?"

"Can't we go to your house, Neve?" Luc turned to me.

I sighed. "You know what will happen if my dad hears us practicing – he'll freak out!" I turned slightly red. I'd still managed to avoid letting Danny Blue know that my dad was Keith Knight, and I wanted to keep it that way as long as possible.

"Your dad not a fan of rock and roll, then?" Danny turned to me with a wry smile.

"He's...uh...old-school," I said. "He's not really a fan of the idea of me being in a band. And we can't use my dorm – I share a room with Kaylee Miller, and you know how she is..."

"I don't want my guitar smelling like pot smoke all week," confirmed Luc. "We could go to my place – but I feel kind of bad, you know? It was one thing when we were kids, but now that we're all off to college Mom's turned the basement into a room for Jennifer so she and Amy don't have to share, and..."

"We could go to my place," said Danny, playing with the keys in his hands.

"Oh, no..." Steve said quickly. "You're new – we don't want to intrude."

"Well, if I'm part of the band – I figure I ought to do my share, right?" Danny's grin managed to make me melt inwardly. "I don't want to be a drag on our resources."

"You're not," I said – too quickly. "I mean – you're already working pretty hard to catch up, and..."

"I *do* have a freezer full of frozen pizzas," Danny added. "And a beach view."

"Those frozen pizzas *do* sound awfully tempting," Steve said. "And it's better than running into Neve's dad..."

"But how are we going to get there?" I said. "The bus doesn't run that late – and everyone knows we can only fit two into Steve's car."

Steve's dad had bought a vintage Volkswagon Beetle for his sixteenth birthday. It looked incredibly cool, but it was also incredibly impractical – there was no way more than three people could fit in at a squeeze. "I left my car on campus – I'd have to walk back to get it..."

"I'll drive Neve," Danny offered. "We've got my car. And then Luc and Kyle and Steve could drive together. You two just follow me..."

The boys looked at each other nervously – as if they

were going to object – and then fell silent. "Yeah, sounds good," said Luc. "You do that." He gave me a wary stare. "You okay with that, Neve?"

"Uh...sure." I was blushing again, wasn't I? I knew it didn't mean anything – Danny was just being gentlemanly by offering to drive me. He wasn't flirting – if that's what the boys were worried about. They knew as well as I did – no dating in the band. Those were the rules – weren't they? Not that Danny Blue – gorgeous, talented, and easily five years my senior, would want anything to do with me.

Still, I couldn't help but feel a shock of electricity as he helped me into his car seat and got in beside me, revving up the engine.

"Still haven't gotten used to driving on the wrong side of the road," he laughed. "Actually, Neve – there's a reason I asked you to come along with me in the car..."

I tensed up, my face going hot and cold all at once. "Oh?"

"I wanted to talk to you about something."

All of a sudden I was painfully aware of his presence beside me; the very air between us seem to hum and vibrate.

"Listen, it doesn't take a genius to figure out that you're in charge here. Of the band, I mean. The others are incredibly talented – but you're clearly the organizer here."

"I guess. The guys like to leave the admin stuff to me – I'm pretty good at it."

"So I trust you completely – if the boys trust you, so do I. But I wanted to get your input on something. I'll go along with whatever you have to say."

"Of course?" What was he talking about?

"We haven't talked about the obvious."

You mean the fact that I'm practically salivating over you?

"Was it that obvious?"

"We haven't met since Monday morning – but tomorrow is class."

"Oh." My face fell. "That."

"I'm still your TA. I've avoided bringing it up because I'm not sure how much of an issue it's going to be. And I'm definitely in for this Friday – you guys needed a guitarist and I'm in. But if, after that, it's weird for you having your TA in your band..."

"Not at all..."

"Ethically, it's put me in a bit of a tight spot. I do

some of the grading for the course, and while I'm sure Professor Poe would understand if I asked him if I could excuse myself from marking your work in particular, I don't want you to feel...obligated."

"I don't – really." I didn't have to think. "We need you here. You're even better than Geoff – though don't let him hear you say that. And the TA stuff – I mean, I'm friends with a few grad students. It's not that weird. It happens. If you can get out of grading my stuff, though, it'd probably be easier..."

"I just don't want you to feel like I'm in a position of power over you," he said.

I'm not sure I'd mind that, I couldn't help thinking. But I only swallowed and nodded. "Believe me, you're not." I said, in a voice that came out cockier than I meant it.

He smiled – a slow, sexy smile that revealed that he was amused. "Well. I'm glad you're a girl who knows how to stay in control."

"I'm good at that."

"Then you won't have a problem coming back to my place, will you?" *Is he flirting? Neve – get a grip – was that flirtation?*

"As long as you haven't got any neighbors to

complain about the noise."

"No neighbors close enough to hear – believe me...I make a *lot* of noise."

This time I was pretty sure he was flirting.

"I'm intrigued."

"I certainly hope you are, Never Ever." He put a hand on my knee and I felt my whole body tingle with anticipation. "You're certainly an intriguing character yourself."

"You think so?" I was aching for him – every fiber of my being calling out for him to touch me again.

"You're a mystery."

I laughed aloud. The tabloids had been covering me ever since I was six years old. "I doubt that very much," I couldn't help saying. "I'm an open book – I can promise you that much. My life's been splashed out on every..."

"Because of your dad?"

So he'd known the whole time. I flushed slightly.

"So you know. That I'm just another celebutante trying to make it big."

"I don't think that about you," he said. "I think if you were, you'd have brought us back to your dad's house – you'd try to capitalize on your name. I haven't seen you doing that. You're a mystery to me, Never." His eyes darkened as they lingered on my face, on my lips. The look he had on his face made my stomach do flip-flops. What I saw in his eyes – was this desire?

He turned abruptly back to the road, stopping the car. "Here we are," he said quickly.

I gasped as I saw his house. Danny lived overlooking the sea, on a tiny remote cottage that looked less like a rock star's pad than like a charming bed and breakfast. Luc, Kyle, and Steve pulled in behind us, and Danny got out of the car, interrupting our interlude.

"Nice place, huh?" Danny said. "I got it for the view. Reminds me of my place in England, near the waterfront."

The house was charming inside and out – simple and rustic, with gorgeous ocean views that seemed even more breathtaking in the moonlight.

"What is this, Ye Olde Seaside Inn?" asked Steve, laughing.

"Mock it all you like," Danny said grinning, "but I bet I can out-rock you any day, paisley curtains or no!"

So we got to jamming. Once again, Danny amazed me – his fingers were so tight, so caressing on the guitar, that watching him play felt like watching a master at work. He knew when to stroke, when to pluck, when to hold – I watched his fingers playing with the string and imagined those hands on my body, against my skin...

I shook my head. *Concentrate, Neve.*

But Danny Blue wasn't making it easy.

Chapter 7

For the next two days, we spent nearly 24/7 practicing at Danny's house. I didn't get much time to follow up our previous conversation. Time was of the essence, and right now we were all business – we barely even had time to exchange "how are you's" and "how are you doings" before settling down to work. And for his part, Danny seemed to have entirely forgotten the flirtatious conversation we'd had in the car – if, indeed, it had been flirtatious at all. His demeanor was stiff – almost cold – something even Kyle and Luc had picked up on, deciding between them that it was due to his Englishness. They'd started calling him "English," to his mild amusement, and cracking jokes about tea and biscuits every opportunity they got. But I couldn't help but wonder if his sudden coolness had something to do with how close we'd gotten – or almost gotten – in the car the week before. I found myself feeling flustered – unable to focus, getting painfully close to distraction, wondering if Danny found me beautiful, found me attractive enough, whether or not he had a girlfriend...questions I'd never asked myself before.

But I didn't have too much time to worry. We had a show to do, and time was running out. Thursday night we rehearsed until three in the morning, and we had only just begun to catch a glimpse of the sunrise on the horizon to the east when at last Danny began to yawn.

"Time to pack up," said Kyle, leaping to his feet. "I'm crashing with Luc and Steve tonight so I don't have such a long commute to campus tomorrow. Neve, do you mind driving yourself back?" This time I'd brought my own car.

"Go on ahead!" I said, bidding farewell to the others and watching as they drove off into the distance. I fumbled with my keys, packing up my equipment and heading into the car.

Bam! No sooner had I started up the car than I felt an unmistakable jolt, followed by a sense of deflation. I'd run over something sharp – who knew what? - and my tire had gone from full to flat in a matter of seconds.

Damn it. I'd been meaning to change the spare tire for weeks, but somehow between the excitement of college and the stress of the band I hadn't been able to make it to the shop. "Guys!" I called out, but they'd already gone. I instinctively picked up my cell phone, ready to dial, before sighing in exasperation. The battery was flat. I'd have to ask Danny for the use of his living room sofa – or else for his car keys – two requests that seemed awfully intimate given our relative coldness. But there was nobody out here for miles – there was no way I could walk back myself. I'd have to ask Danny...

Flushing with embarrassment, I made my way back to Danny's house. I knocked softly, but I heard no reply.

"Danny?" I called out. I followed the lights into his bedroom, but stopped on the threshold, embarrassed. Danny was sitting on the bed, entirely naked except for a towel, his hair soaking wet, playing on his acoustic guitar, which had drowned out my words.

I turned bright pink and stepped back. It was awkward enough walking in on my TA at 4 in the morning – did he have to be naked, too? My heart was fluttering faster than one of Steve's beats – if Danny's muscle tees suggested chiseled, ripped, abs, they certainly didn't do him proper justice; now that he was shirtless, I could tell that Danny was easily the most toned guy I'd ever met. His skin glistened and across his chest and one shoulder was some kind of medieval pattern tattoo. Over his heart, there was a large lion's head in blue. From this distance I couldn't see the entire pattern or make out the words scrawled beneath it across his lower stomach leading down to the v hidden by his towel slung loosely low on his hips. I gulped. As much as I tried, I couldn't take my eyes off of him. Danny Blue made wearing clothes to cover up that gorgeous body a sin. *Why does he have to be so hot?*

He was playing a haunting song on the guitar.

"Danny..." I whispered – but as soon as I caught sight of his face I fell silent. His eyes were red, and tears were streaming down his face. He was singing...

> *"Since I lost you/I've never known*
> *how to feel anything but alone*
> *Since you're gone – all I can see*
> *An empty road in front of me..."*

His voice grew ragged and rough with his tears; he closed his eyes and kept on playing.

> *"I can't see the rest of it through*
> *knowing I'm living without you*

One year today – and it's still not real
One year today – I cannot heal..."

He stopped playing, and in a fury pushed his guitar to the floor. It clattered loudly – and I stepped back, embarrassed. I didn't want him to know I'd seen him like this. Better to spend the night in my car...

I tiptoed backwards towards the door, hoping I wouldn't disturb him. Maybe if I just knocked again, more loudly, he'd think I'd just arrived. I waited a few minutes before I cleared my throat loudly and knocked again at the front door.

This time all the lights were off. He must have gone to sleep. But I couldn't wait any longer. Already I was hazy on my feet, half-asleep with exhaustion. I needed to get some sleep – I was dead tired and I needed to be in top form for tomorrow. I crept back into his bedroom, praying that I'd be able to wake him up without touching him.

I stumbled my way towards him, not able to see much except in the darken room except the outline of his bed and him in it. "Danny..." I whispered. "Danny, wake up..."

I caught sight of his towel on the floor near his bed,

almost tripping on it – he must have gone to bed completely naked. The thought filled me with a mixture of embarrassment and desire, remembering what I had seen of him just moments before. "Danny..."

I didn't want to do this, but I didn't have a choice. I reached out to touch him, tapping his shoulder. "Danny, I'm really sorry, but..."

He groaned lightly. "You..." he murmured. "I've been missing you..."

My heart skipped a beat. *Danny Blue had missed me.*

He reached out and pulled me to him. "You feel so soft," he murmured, resting his head against my stomach. "You smell so good...."

"Danny, wake..."

I wanted to say something, but no sooner had I opened my mouth than he pulled me onto the bed and stopped it with a kiss. Instantly my mind went blank – the touch was electric, overwhelming. The smell of him was intoxicating.

Nobody in the band, Neve...

But feeling Danny Blue with his arms around me was too good to resist. I couldn't push him away now. So –

he'd wanted me, too. As much as I had wanted him. It had felt right...in my sleep-deprived state I was no longer sure whether I was asleep or awake. All I knew was that his lips tasted so good on mine. I'd wanted him for so long. *And he wanted me too.*

He threw an arm across my body, pinning me in place.

"Danny..." I tried to say. "I need your keys..." But I was so tired, so sleepy, that the words wouldn't come. Before I knew it, I was asleep in his arms, his naked body warm and sweaty against my own.

I woke up to the light streaming in through the window, and the smell of the salty sea air. *Where was I?* And then I remembered. I was in Danny's bed – we'd kissed – we'd fallen asleep side by side. I looked over at him – he'd turned away from me in the middle of the night, his hair tousled with sleep, his long dark lashes fanned out on his chiseled cheekbones. Even in sleep he looked beautiful, like a fallen angel – his face strangely vulnerable without the cocky arrogance that gave him such an irresistible presence during the day. Tears were still wet upon his pillow. What had made him suffer so, I wondered? What gave him such pain? I wanted to reach over and touch his face, to kiss his full sexy lips, to wipe away the wetness that glistened from tears of pain clinging to his lashes. He looked so vulnerable, so much like a lost little boy. I glanced down at myself. I was fully clothed, but my hand was resting underneath the covers against Danny's hard stomach, below his waist.

Oh God, what did I just do...

Maybe we could pretend it never happened. Maybe...

I tried to sneak out of bed, but he turned in his sleep and threw his arm over me again. "No..." he whispered, still half-asleep, "don't go...I always sleep better with you..."

Wait, what?

"Danny..." my voice began to falter."

"No..." he murmured. "Stay with me, Peyton..."

My eyes widened. "Peyton?" I couldn't resist exclaiming out loud, so loudly that his eyes shot open. "Who's *Peyton?*"

He sprang to his feet, shock and panic spreading across his face, as he grabbed a pillow to cover himself.

"Neve? *What the hell are you doing here?*"

Chapter 8

I was turning several shades of bright scarlet as Danny's eyebrows crinkled in confusion. It was abundantly clear that Danny Blue had no idea whatsoever what had happened between us last night. The look of warmth on his face – the soft cadence of his voice – all these had vanished, replaced by a look of utter surprise. If it were anyone else – if it were Kyle or Luc or Steve – I'd know how to handle it. We'd fallen asleep next to each other before and sometimes even woken up cuddling (hell, even Luc and Steve had woken up together a time or two). We'd always just laughed it off, chalked it up to drink or exhaustion – but this was different. I'd spent the night wrapped up in Danny Blue's arms, fantasizing about his skin against mine, about his hands trailing up and down my body – under the impression that he, at least, fantasizing about me too.

"I'm...so sorry..." I stuttered, trying to think as quickly as I could. If he didn't remember what happened between us, I figured, at least I could find a way to spin things that wasn't so awkward. "My car broke down last night...I wanted to wake you...couldn't...slept on the couch..."

"*Your car broke down?*"

"Isleptonthecouch," I said breathlessly, trying to force the words out of my mouth. "I was stranded last night – I mean, this morning. And I couldn't get home and my phone was dead so I went back in to find you but you were asleep, and, uh..."

"Unclad?" Danny couldn't help but betray a hint of a smile. One hell of a sexy smile. The image of his gorgeous, chiseled naked body was distracting, even now. He grabbed a luscious green silk dressing gown and put it on. "No, you wouldn't have been able to wake me up – even if you'd wanted to." His eyes darkened. "I've been on prescription sleeping medication for...well, just about a year now. Had an accident. Helps me sleep. Once I take one of those, I'm knocked out for the night – completely unconscious."

Not completely, I thought.

"I didn't have anywhere to go," I explained. "I didn't want to bother you so I figured I'd just sleep on the couch."

"It's not your fault," said Danny. "I sleep like the

dead even at the best of times – and with three hours average of sleep two days running, I'm out like a light. I've been running on adrenaline for days now. But had I known, I would of course have gotten up and driven you back home. I am a gentleman, after all. Even if last night I was a very sleepy, very conked-out gentleman. I hope you'll forgive me. Was the couch comfortable, at least?"

I could still smell the sweet smell of vanilla and cinnamon in his hair. "Very."

"Well, let's talk about all this over a good old fry-up, shall we? Only – er, Neve?"

"What?"

"I *do* need to get dressed at some point."

Shame. "Of course," I was even more flustered than before. "I'll, just, uh – well, I'll wait in the living room, okay?"

I sat on his living room couch, looking out at the sea, unsure of how to feel. On the one hand, I was relieved that Danny apparently remembered nothing of our midnight adventure, and didn't think I was some kind of crazed stalker or rapist intent on getting into his bed at all costs. On the other hand, it meant that those kind words Danny had said, his caressing tone of voice, his kisses and the words he'd used – they weren't for me. They were for his dream girl, the girl whose name he'd cried out in the early hours of the morning – *Peyton*...I should have known. He probably had a girlfriend. Someone like Danny Blue was mature, worldly, sophisticated. What could he see in a bright-eyed college freshman like me?

He emerged from the bedroom a few minutes later, shiny and showered, his black jeans showing off the shape of his hips, a businesslike black blazer over a decidedly grungy white tee, and a corded leather masculine necklace around his neck. He looked like a fashion model stepping out of the magazine. "Sit," he said, pointing to one of the large stools at the kitchen's island counter. His voice was firm – I almost bristled at the easy authority with which he assumed over me; he sounded like the TA Mr. Blue, not the friendly, sexy Danny I knew. But somehow I didn't mind. I sat at the kitchen counter while Danny loaded up a frying pan full of bacon, mushroom, eggs, and sausages.

"Great hangover cure from back home," Danny said, "but it also works to give you energy if you haven't slept."

"I'm not hungry..." I tried to protest, feeling I'd already intruded enough.

"We've got a gig tonight," said Danny. "You need your strength – and so do I. Besides, the eggs are going off today and I need someone to help me eat them."

He plopped down two plates on the kitchen countertop. I was still too nervous to eat, and only vaguely picked at my eggs, still feeling like an alien in Danny's strange world, wishing I could get out of there, away from Danny, away from the distracting image of Danny's naked body that refused to leave my head.

"Tsk tsk!" he noted. "You're not touching your bacon. I'm almost hurt, Neve. I drive all the way to the butcher's twenty miles from here to get proper English bacon done right – won't you at least tell me if you like it?"

"I'm good," I muttered.

"Oh, for goodness' sake, you're not one of those girls who just eats salad and lettuce, are you? Given how much energy you expend singing I always figured you just had a fast metabolism. Tell me you're not on a diet, please!" He laughed and waved a fork full of bacon in my face. "When I was little my mum used to tell me to open up for the "choo choo train". I'm not going to have to do that with you, am I? Because I know from experience – salad does not sufficient energy make for a night of performance."

"I'm not on a diet!" I protested. "It's just that bacon makes me break out – and the last thing I want to do before tonight is show up with pimples all over my face."

Danny shrugged. "Your loss," he said, and finished the bacon himself. It smelled delicious – but I couldn't stand the thought of eating right now when my stomach was doing flip flops. "I wouldn't worry so much if I were you. Your skin's fine – really, it's flawless. Either you put on a hell of a lot of makeup before I woke up this morning, or you're worrying too much..."

I flushed pink, enjoying the compliment – even if it was disguised in a healthy dose of teasing. "I've got youth to thank," I said, "but my mom always says that by the time I hit thirty...." *Crap, why did I have to say thirty? Danny must be a few years shy of thirty.* Why did I have to remind him just how young I was – he'd probably already pulled away, after that first night of rehearsals, after realizing I was only eighteen. Why did I have to make things worse?

Danny only smiled. "You are pretty young, aren't you? But someone would think you were at least thirty – given how busy you are, and how you're able to manage a group of guys so well. Your age hasn't stopped you from getting out there, doing things..."

"I guess it's because my parents started young," I said, calming down somewhat now that Danny and I were both clothed and carrying a conversation like two normal people.

"It sounds like an interesting upbringing," said Danny, crossing his arms, "and one day I'd love to sit down with you and talk all about it. But right now I don't think it's the time – you – and I for that matter – have to get to Professor Poe's class in thirty minutes, and if we don't hurry, we'll be late. There's a guest bedroom and bath through the hall – you can use the spare toothbrush in there if you like...."

I hurried through breakfast, brushing my teeth and washing my face as quickly as I could. Unfortunately, last night's makeup was still smeared on my face, and my clothes were decidedly – embarassingly – slept-in. Even Danny Blue's meticulously-kept guest bathroom – as clean and well-stocked as a hotel lavatory – couldn't keep me from looking like I was doing anything but the walk of shame.

"Knock knock!" Danny entered with a pile of clothes in his arms. "I had these lying around – I thought you might want to change into something. I mean – as lovely as the "day old" look is, I figured you'd want something that didn't smell of Steve's spilled beer."

"Thanks," I said, taking them. I wanted to know where they came from – did Danny have a girlfriend? - but I didn't mention it.

Luckily, the clothes fit me just fine. When I emerged into the living room, however, Danny turned pale – a look of absolute shock spreading over his face, as if he'd seen a ghost.

"Is something wrong?" I asked him.

"No..." he couldn't look at me. "No...it's fine. They – uh, they suit you. You look nice." But from his expression, I knew something was wrong – and I knew just as surely that it wasn't up to me to ask. Danny Blue was getting more and more mysterious by the minute.

Chapter 9

Danny and I were mostly silent as he drove me to class. We stared straight ahead, keeping our eyes on the road, looking out at the sea that lapped at the feet of the cliffs.

"Er, Neve? I don't mean to be awkward..." he began. Of course, with that melting English accent of his and those piercing sapphire-colored eyes, he couldn't be awkward even if he wanted to.

"Sure?" I looked over at him.

"I'm new as a TA to this class," he said, "and I want to make a good impression on Professor Poe, especially if I'll be going up for teaching jobs at the end of the year once I submit my dissertation."

"Sure?"

"And I'd really rather not – not that of course you don't know the truth – but, I don't want to make a bad impression, or risk my reputation..."

I realized what he was getting at. If I turned up on

campus early in the morning in Danny Blue's car, people might think we'd slept together. People might *know*, rather, that we'd slept together – in a manner of speaking. And that would be pretty damaging to Danny's career, not to mention my own reputation.

"So do you mind if I drop you off on campus here and you walk the rest of the way?"

"Sure..." I said, feeling relieved to have a few seconds to myself to deal with my thoughts. My heart was still racing as I left the car and jogged across campus; I needed to expel all this energy, all this pent-up frustration, that was coursing through me. *What were you thinking, girl?* What *had* I been thinking? I'd succumbed to the temptation of a moment, to Danny's glorious body and his soft, sweet words – I'd risked the integrity of the band and my friendship with the boys for a night that hadn't even gone anywhere, which Danny didn't even notice or remember. No, this couldn't happen again – even if Danny wanted it to, which from his relatively formal demeanor I was pretty sure he didn't. I had to stay strong, stay professional. I had to stay away from Danny Blue.

But when I arrived in class mere seconds after he did – when our eyes met from across the room and he shot me the tiniest hint of a secret smile – I knew that it would be hard. The past few days had been a crash course in Danny-ology, and now I knew it would be hard to keep ourselves to the teacher/student relationship we needed to maintain in the classroom. I felt close to him – strangely possessive of him – and I couldn't look at him in that tight-fitting black blazer without being able to make out the tantalizing forms of the muscles underneath. I wanted him – I knew that – my whole body ached to be close to him, to be with him as I'd never been with – or even wanted to be with – anyone else before. I'd heard his music – I'd heard the mysterious, plaintive song he'd written and played in secret, the tears streaming down his face as he played. I felt that I'd looked through a window into his soul – that we were connected by some strange bond, by the power of the music that he played, and the music that I sang. There was still so much to learn about him – who was Peyton? Why did he still cry when he sang about her? And why had he freaked out when he saw me in that set of clothes – clothes that still seemed to unnerve him every time his eyes fell upon me in the classroom?

Nobody else seemed to notice the distraction, however. As soon as Danny got up to speak – lecturing about the relationship of goth rock to post-punk in Northern England – the entire class was lapping out of the palm of his hand. Even the stoners and the jocks taking this course for an easy A were leaning in, excited by his words – his fluid, smooth delivery. He didn't just lecture; he told *stories* – talking to us about Ian Curtis and Joy Division and New Order, about the clubs of Manchester and Siouxsie Sioux's first performance that were so full of detail and color that it almost seemed as if he had been there.

Of course, his looks would have more than sufficed even if his teaching style hadn't been up to snuff. The other girls were giggling and staring at him; one girl, raising her arm in a pointed way designed to thrust forth her bosom, asked a question about Ian Curtis' sex life clearly designed to get him to notice her. And when Danny smiled at her, charmingly answering her question while deflecting any talk about sex, I couldn't help but feel a twinge of jealousy.

It was a relief to get out when class ended.

"Neve!" Danny called, using the formal professor-voice that still managed to send tingles up and down my side. "May I see you for a moment?"

"Of course, sir!" I called out cheerily, feeling a frisson of excitement at this game we were playing – the teacher-student relationship hiding our closer intimacy.

"I'll see you tonight," he said quietly, so that Professor Poe wouldn't hear. "I've got a lot of meetings and classes to teach, so I won't be there early, but I will be there." He touched my shoulder slightly so that I shivered. "If I'm a bit late, don't worry. I will be there no matter what – I won't let you down."

"Thanks," I said, smiling at him. "We'll be great, I know it. You'll be great. I'll see you tonight." I instinctively leaned in, my arms tensed to hug him – an automatic response I'd learned after several experiences with Luc, Kyle, Steve, and Geoff – but I stopped myself at once, my body remembering the feeling of his body against mine, of his arms twined with my own, of his muscular chest tight against my back. I couldn't touch him without becoming overwhelmed with feelings of how much I wanted him, wanted to be close to him, wanted his body so close against mine. I had to watch myself, to keep my feelings – not to mention my hormones – under control.

"Bye," I said awkwardly, all but rushing out of the classroom.

That afternoon I ran into Kyle after our shared Calculus requirement. He was strangely cold to me during class – but it was only after the bell rang that I found out why.

"Knocked on your door," he said curtly. "Way to stand me up this morning."

What? And then I remembered. My standing Friday morning breakfast date with Kyle. I'd completely forgotten.

"Nobody was in – your roommate said you hadn't come back last night." Kyle frowned. "Really, you could have called if you weren't going to come back – not to mention...did you spend the night at Danny's? Really, Neve, after everything you said about Geoff, I can't believe you'd..."

"I got a flat!" I blurted, hoping Kyle wouldn't see my red face. "Nothing happened. I couldn't get home so I slept on the couch because I was so exhausted. Danny offered to drive me home but it was too late, so he just drove me in this morning."

Kyle looked relieved – a little *too* relieved, I thought. "Good," he said – before turning slightly crimson. "Because you know, uh, I promised your mom I'd look out for you. There's no way she'd let you live in the dorms instead of at home if she didn't think I'd keep you out of any trouble." He coughed slightly.

I patted his hands. "Don't worry, Kyle," I said. "I'd never screw with the band dynamic like that – you know that. You can trust me. Nothing happened. You know as well as I do that I'd never date anyone in the band."

"I know that," Kyle said. "And you know that. All too well. But does Danny know that?"

Does he? I looked hurriedly at the floor so that Kyle wouldn't be able to see my face. *And for that matter – do I?*

That night, the boys and I drove together to the night club, planning to meet Danny there. I was expecting him to turn up in his typical rock star regalia – but when Danny showed up, it was all I could do not to melt into a puddle on the floor then and there. He was wearing skin-tight leather trousers and a black silk button-down shirt that opened all the way to his navel, revealing his toned chest and killer abs. The blue stud in his ear matched the piercing color of his icy eyes; his hair was slicked back to his shoulders.

I shuddered with desire.

But none of that – nothing about his looks – could compare to his playing. The second Danny's lithe fingers touched the guitar strings, he was making love not only to me, but to every single woman in the room. His desire, his longing, his sexy cocksure style – all these seemed to echo through the room with his playing, making the walls shake. I sang along with his melody, our voices and instruments blending into one another, melding together to create a lush wall of sound, overwhelming and gorgeous. I couldn't breathe; somehow, I could sing anyway, energy coursing through us both. Normally, the adrenaline sent me spinning – but tonight was something different, something profound. The normal energy of performance mingled with my desire for Danny – a desire that caused my whole body to shudder like a guitar string. We weren't just giving a great performance tonight – we were giving a performance that was out of this world! I could feel it – Danny could feel it – Luc and Steve and Kyle could feel it. We had our audience by the throats and we weren't going to let them go. We'd drawn them in; we'd seduced them. We were going to make love to them and bring them back wanting more.

Between my desire and Danny's talent – his presence had brought the Never Knights to a whole new level.

I couldn't focus with him near me. But as we finished the set, the audience exploding with applause, I knew the band couldn't function with us apart, either.

Kailin Gow

Chapter 10

By the time we played our last song of the night, I was absolutely exhausted – my mind and body alike completely shattered. But as the music died down, I spied something out of the corner of my eye that made my heart start to race anew: Mr. Slayton was sitting at one of the corner tables, a curious expression on his face. So, Slayton was serious after all, I thought, my face turning red with excitement. Apparently he thought our band had potential after all. Well, if he'd seen us tonight, then he'd seen exactly how much energy Danny Blue had injected into our proceedings. He didn't just have the raw talent of a Geoff – he had technique as well, skill and dedication. Exactly what Slayton was looking for. My face was flushed with pleasure – I was so glad he'd seen us tonight, of all nights. I cleared my throat and started announcing the band members.

"We're the Never Knights. I'm Neve Knight..."

"Hold on!" I heard some shouting and turned

around. "Hey, you, stand back!" Luc was growling as Kyle and Steve tried to hold off a young, gawky guy holding a cell phone camera.

"Hey, what are you..."

But before I could respond, the young man leaped onto the stage, grabbed me, and forced a kiss on me, shoving his tongue down my throat before I even knew what was happening. I heard a cold "*click*" - the sound of his cell phone camera recording the moment.

Instinctively, I shoved him away, horror spreading over my face. *Quick, Neve, play it cool*, I told myself, but my whole body was recoiling in disgust. I felt sick, violated – that this guy could run onstage and assault me like that. But I couldn't let the crowd see me upset. "Looks like we've got some dedicated fans, huh?" I forced myself to say, and the crowd laughed.

But the guy who had kissed me – currently being held by Steve and Kyle, who looked ready to pummel him at any moment – didn't seem too bothered. "Keith Knight's daughter!" he was shouting, completely drunk, "I kissed Keith Knight's daughter! Whoo!"

I heard several more *clicks* from the crowd, as one by one, people took photos with their phones. My stomach plummeted. I'd tried to keep my identity – if not an outright secret – then pretty damn quiet. I didn't play the Keith Knight's daughter card – if anything, I wanted my dad to know nothing of my dreams to follow in his footsteps. But I knew what came next – I'd seen it happen to plenty of my friends, other celebrities' kids. First the camera-phone shot, then the feature on TMZ or Perez Hilton – by tomorrow, the entire Internet would be seeing and laughing at my embarrassing moment, caught on film. Not to mention my dad. And once he found out about the band, I knew, he'd freak out. It was what I was most afraid of. The fame I wanted – the way I didn't want it to happen. I'd be a laughingstock, a celebutante. Not the serious artist I wanted to be.

"Hey..." Kyle handed me a bottle of ice-cold water as we left the stage. "Are you okay?" He put his arm around me.

"It's just a kiss, Kyle," I said with more bravado than I felt. "No big deal, believe me."

"No big deal?" Kyle's mouth opened into a wide-O. "That guy just sexually assaulted you – I'm pretty sure you could press charges if you wanted to."

"This crapola happens."

"Crapola? Shit, Neve, why don't you let it all out? It's got no right to happen. It doesn't matter that you're in a band, that you're Keith Knight's daughter – nobody should have to be groped by complete strangers. He had no right to kiss you like that – no right at all." Kyle's face was redder than mine.

"It's not that he kissed me..." I admitted. "That's not what freaks me out. It's just that – if he could get that close, if he could get close enough to shove his tongue down my throat – what else could he have done...?" Images shot through my mind of famous rock stars and their kids who'd been killed or threatened by psychos off the street – John Lennon, shot down in front of the Dakota....

"Look, Neve," said Kyle. "I promised your mom I'd look after you. I know that people want something from you – that when you're a rock star's kid you get special kind of surveillance. But don't worry." He set his jaw. "There won't be a next time for a case like that. I won't let it happen again."

"Hey, Neve," Steve came over. "I just had a few...uh...choice words with security. They're pretty sorry – they apologize profusely and say that it won't happen again. It's bad publicity for them – worse than for us. This isn't supposed to be some frat-bar – this is one of the hottest, most elegant clubs in town. Unfortunately, that guy already emailed the video clip of himself kissing you to TMZ...”

My heart almost skipped a beat. *Here it is*, I thought. *The fame and fortune you never wanted.* The fame and fortune I'd always known, deep down, I could never avoid. Not as Keith Knight's daughter – who, incidentally, still wasn't even old enough to technically be in this nightclub.

“He's bound to find out, then,” I sighed. “My dad. I just hoped he wouldn't find out until we're already signed...”

Luc rushed over to me, his arms around me, holding me tight. “Oh, babe, I'm so sorry,” he said. “How are you doing?”

“Fine...” I didn't want to go over this again. “It was just a kiss – nothing else.”

“Please...” Luc pressed his lips to my forehead. “This is just a kiss – this right here. A normal thing that happens between friends. What that guy did to you wasn't a kiss – it was assault. A complete stranger who thinks he has the right to...”

I smiled into Luc's warm, protective eyes. “You're

more worried than I am," I said. "Believe me, I can handle myself. But I think one kiss cancels out the other. You made me feel a lot better, thanks."

He put on a pretend falsetto voice. "Kissing away the boo-boo?" he laughed, thrusting out his bosom in a failed attempt to look maternal. "Like when we were playing house as kids?"

"I *wish* Neve's mom would 'kiss away the boo boo'," Kyle laughed. "I'd get injured a lot more if she were the one doing the bandaging."

"You guys..." I laughed too. "I think we're a little too old for 'a kiss will make it better.'"

Luc chuckled. "You never know," he said. "A kiss can cure a lot of ills. It's true. Great for the common cold..." He fixed his gaze on me – warm and loving.

"Luc..." His face was so kind, so familiar – yet there was something about it that was foreign to me, even strange. Somehow Luc had grown up right under my nose, from a great childhood friend to a wonderful, caring man – from a gawky boy to a handsome adult. How had I never noticed this change before?

"Don't worry about me, Luc," I said. "I bet a bunch of those girls out there on the dance floor would be happy to have a guy like you go kiss away all *their* injuries."

"Believe it or not," Luc said, brushing my cheek lightly with his hand. "None of that matters. What matters is you. I wanted to make sure that you were okay – that's my priority right now." He smiled into my face, holding my hands tight.

"Hello – Neve?" The voice sent tingles down my spine as Danny approached, a strange expression on his face as he looked me and Luc up and down. For a moment I saw something strange in his eyes – a flash of darkness, a moment of pain. That brooding expression that made me think, again, of Lord Byron.

"Oh..." I realized how it must look – me and Luc in each other's arms – and I swiftly pulled away. "Danny..." Danny was the only one of us who didn't know just how adamant my dad was that I stay out of the rock scene – let alone be in a rock band. Who didn't know just how afraid my dad was that I'd fall into the same traps he fell into – a life of meaningless sex, drugs, and booze that had nearly killed him. "Great job, Danny!"

"Thanks," he flushed slightly. "I should say the same for you and the rest of the band. Not that I have to. This guy looks like he's going to say the same thing..."

Mr. Slayton approached us.

"Mr. Slayton!" I tried to sound bright and professional. "You're here. Thank you so much for coming back, for checking us out again..."

"You really have improved," he said, nodding approvingly. "Already I could tell the difference in the sound, and it's only been a week."

I looked over at Danny. "We've got a new lead," I said. "I think he's done a lot to inspire all of us to work harder."

"Yes, I know Mr. Blue," said Mr. Slayton. "We've met before. I'm glad you have him on board – his style really does add something to your performance. This is a step up from the Veridium, for sure..."

"Thanks," I said, looking at Danny, feeling the excitement radiate from my eyes.

"But that stunt with the camera..." Mr. Slayton continued. "It really made me aware of just how cautious I have to be signing a band like yours. You're not just some ingenue, Miss Knight; you're Keith Knight's daughter, whether you want to be or not. And that means that when do you break into the business, the attention on you will be huge. Expectations will be higher – you'll naturally invite comparisons, scrutiny. And I'm not willing to put you out there, to sign you, unless I've got complete faith that you're not going to be just a passing fad. I want you to be more than just a rocker's daughter, Neve – I want this band to stand or fall on its own merits. And that means I'm going to have to be cautious. I'm not saying "no," Neve – but I am saying I want to wait a while before putting you – or any of your band mates – into the spotlight."

He held out his hand to me and I shook it. "Thank you for your faith, Mr. Slayton," I said. "We'll only improve." I looked over at Danny. "We're sure to."

"You're on the right track," said Mr. Slayton, "keep it up." He shook everyone's hand and left. No sooner had he gone than the club manager, looking flushed and apologetic in her black dress, came up to us. "I'm so sorry for what happened tonight – that guy was clearly high; he should never have made it past the bouncers. Our security had – uh – a talk with him afterward, and he's been banned from this hotel. His name is John Flint – and he won't be bothering you anymore. But we here at the Imperial Hotel want to make up for it anyway. We hope that this will go some way towards making up for the trouble. If you'll just follow me..."

She led us out of the night club and into the hotel upstairs of which the club was part, into a gorgeous lush VIP lounge filled with buckets of ice, steaming bottles of champagne, and a tantalizing looking wine and cheese spread. The room was filled with women – a few I recognized as the wives or daughters of some of the biggest record execs in the business – all of whom had eyes only for our band members. Kyle and Steve, eyeing girls they knew, were soon lost in conversation with a pair of stunning models.

"Pity they didn't bring some guys for you," Danny laughed in my ear. "Gender equality and all that."

"I've had enough strangers kiss me for one night, thanks," I said.

The manager turned to me and Danny. "We're also happy to put you up in some of our finest rooms tonight," she said, glancing at Danny. "If you'll just tell me how many you need." Her eyes traveled from me to Danny, and back again, her question implicit: *how many rooms? Are you two sleeping together, or separately?* I couldn't help but catch Danny's eye, knowing all the while what it felt like to sleep with his naked body against my own...

"Neve," Danny started. "I wanted to talk to..."

But before he could finish his sentence, a gaggle of girls let loose a cry. "There he is!" Immediately Danny was swarmed by a crowd of gorgeous women – all asking for his autograph, giving him their numbers. Among them was Amber, the drop-dead gorgeous blonde from our class.

"Amber," Danny gave her his trademark dazzling smile. "So good to see you." He leaned in close and whispered something into her ear, which made her in turn chirp with laughter. I couldn't help it. White-hot jealousy surged through me. I had to restrain the impulse to leap onto Amber, to claw at her, to pull her off Danny...

I had to get out of there. I couldn't let my emotions compromise me – compromise the band. Not when Slayton was keeping us under such close tabs. *This is why you promised never to date anyone in the band*, I told myself. *No complications*. If I started a relationship with Danny – with anybody – this jealousy, these feelings, would only get worse.

I left the champagne and elegance behind and walked off onto the hotel's veranda. I needed to be alone.

But I felt hopeless, trapped. I'd spent so long trying to keep my feelings and personal life out of the band. But now, I knew, I had no choice. I was head over heels for

Danny Blue.

And that meant we were all headed for disaster.

Chapter 11

The moon was full and the night was cold. As I stepped out into the shadowy night, I had never felt lonelier. I should be feeling great about tonight – everything had started off so well. Slayton was impressed; we'd played better than ever; the audience was eating out of our hands. But instead I felt exhausted, hopeless. My feelings for Danny were messing with my head – and with those photos of me headed straight for the Internet, there was no way in hell I'd be able to escape my dad hearing all about the Never Knights in a matter of hours. I still felt furious about that stalker, John Flint. Violated, even. I'd put on a brave face in front of the guys, but deep down I was disgusted – disgusted and ashamed. By getting up onstage to kiss me, by filming it for all the world to see, he was saying out loud what I'd always been afraid of hearing, what I'd told myself in my darkest moments: "don't take her seriously – she's just a celebrity's kid. She's tabloid fodder, not the real thing." Was that what Slayton thought of me now – just another "famous for being famous" wannabe without the talent to back up her blind ambition? I sighed, looking up at the moon mournfully. "If I were a wolf I would howl," I muttered sadly.

Did my father ever have to deal with crazed stalkers like that? Did my mother? If my dad thought the rock and roll business was no place for his daughter before, he'd certainly think so after...I decided. I had to call home right away. Better they hear about what happened from me directly than read it in the morning papers. I picked up my phone to dial, but a rustling sound from behind distracted me.

Danny was emerging from the shadows, the moonlight making his gorgeous smooth skin shine incandescently before me as the shadows vanished from his face. In his black leather, in this moonlight, he looked a little like a vampire, I thought. One sexy vampire at that. Well, if he was, I thought to myself grimly, I wasn't doing a good job of running away. I knew that he meant danger, and yet here I was, standing – waiting for the kill.

"Hey," he said softly. "I wanted to talk to you after...what happened. But that horde of women came after me and by the time I got away you were gone."

"Poor baby," I rolled my eyes and tried to laugh. "Getting surrounded by a bevy of gorgeous women. I see you had no problem leaving them behind."

He shrugged and smiled that self-deprecating smile that seemed to shoot right through my heart.

"Been there," he said airily. "Done that. I directed them in Kyle and Steve's direction. That sort of thing's not my scene. It hasn't been my scene for a long time. That part of being in a band doesn't interest me."

I was surprised to hear it. If my dad – not to mention my band mates – were anything to go by, that was precisely the most interesting part of being a band. "You're a surprise, Danny," I said. "I figured all rockers liked having groupies around."

"Not me," said Danny. "I'm a one-woman kind of guy. Or was."

"Good," I said, automatically, before realizing what I'd said and turning scarlet. "I mean – after what happened to Geoff. The last time he hit on a girl he ended up falling through a glass coffee table. One less potential casualty for me to worry about."

"Neve," Danny said softly, looking worried. "I've been meaning to ask you – you know, if you're okay and everything. I saw what that guy did to you. I know you're putting on a brave face, but if you feel shaken or upset – I just wanted to talk to you about it. But I saw Slayton coming over to you and figured I'd distract him while you got your composure back. Didn't want him to see you at anything but your best."

Danny was being a lot sweeter than he'd been earlier that morning. Did he care about me after all? "Thanks," I couldn't resist smiling. "I didn't think you'd do that."

"Do what?"

"Worry about me."

"Why wouldn't I?" Danny fixed his blue eyes on mine. "I'm part of the band now, aren't I? So I care about being part of this team; I care about everything that affects the band, one way or the other."

I bit back my disappointment. So this wasn't about me – or caring about me. Danny cared about the band, which meant he cared about me as long as I could sing. He probably wasn't interested in me at all. Maybe he was into blondes like Amber – or else his heart belonged to the mysterious Peyton, whoever she was...

"Oh, well," I said, trying to sound casual. "That's

nice."

Danny smiled softly. "Nice?" he said. "Or bland?"

"What do you mean?" He was standing so close that we were practically touching.

"Neve, I'm not blind, you know."

"What are you talking about?" I could feel the heat rising to my face.

"Every time we're in the same room together – this weird...thing we need to resolve, you and I. To get past it. So we can work together." The air between us crackled with electricity; I couldn't bear the tension a moment longer. "Neve, I haven't played in a band for a long time. And it feels good to belong to one again. I don't want to jeopardize that. But when we talk – you remind me so much of her, Neve..." he lightly touched my chin.

"Of who?" My mind was all over the place; all I could concentrate on was the feeling of his fingers against my chin.

"Peyton," he said.

Peyton again. "Who is she...?"

"My..." he swallowed hard. "My girlfriend."

"Oh." Disappointment flooded over me. "I should...I should go..." I felt furious, repulsed. Not only was Danny taken, he was apparently the kind of guy who would cheat on his girlfriend if the moment came up – the kind of guy who would touch another girl's chin, looking at her all the while like he wanted to touch a lot more than that...

"Neve, wait..." Danny protested. "I'm not explaining this right. It's just – it's hard to talk about. But we need to talk about it. I don't want to scare you off, Neve. Steve told me about what happened with Geoff, about your rules. You don't want to date anyone in the band – and especially not Geoff. And if I'm making a complete tit of myself and you haven't been feeling anything at all for me then please just tell me now so I can stop talking..."

"No, don't stop," I couldn't help saying.

"I don't want to be like Geoff. But I can't help feeling...maybe you want me to be?"

"It's just a complicated time," I said. "It's not just about Geoff. With RRR and Slayton and everything..."

"I wouldn't worry about Slayton," said Danny. "He's a great guy once you get to know him."

"And you do?" I was distracted by my shock. How had Danny Blue gotten to know the face behind the hottest music label in town?

Danny turned crimson. "He used to represent me," he said. "When I was in another band."

"What happened to it?"

"Peyton," he said darkly. "Neve..."

"So you broke up?" I couldn't help asking. "You're not together anymore?"

"You could say that."

So, Danny had already dissolved one band due to a break-up....

"Nobody wanted to be in that band anymore," Danny said. "Not after..." He took a breath. "Neve, Peyton died this time last year. Car crash."

So that was Danny Blue's secret. The secret that made those gorgeous blue eyes fill with pain and rage and darkness. The source of his tears, of his haunting music.

I was torn between sadness and relief – grief for Danny's grief, and shameful, ecstatic relief....that Danny wasn't with anyone else, that Peyton was a thing of the past. I flushed, ashamed at my own thoughts, trying to make sense of how I felt.

"I'm so sorry, Danny..." I was holding him, hugging him as I would hug Luc or Kyle when I wanted to comfort him, "Danny, I didn't know."

He reached up and grabbed my hand, hard. For a moment I thought he was pushing me away. And then I saw the hard, naked look of desire in his eyes.

"I can't take this another second, Neve," he said in a hoarse voice, grabbing me by the wrists and leading me back inside, into the elevator.

"Where are you going?" I looked up at him, confused. "What are we doing?"

"We've got to do something about this, Neve. Get it out of our systems. Before it gets the better of both of us. We have to resolve this – or else we're never going to be able to concentrate. If we just act on it – get it out of the way – maybe we won't....Neve, since Peyton died I haven't so much looked at another girl. I haven't wanted to. But with you – I feel something. This chemistry… I can't stand it." He pressed me against the elevator walls, his lips slamming against mine. "If these bloody elevators don't hurry up I swear I'm not accountable for whatever happens next."

I could feel my own body tensed, set aflame by his desire.

The elevator opened and Danny rushed me down the corridor, hurriedly unlocking the suite door.

"What comes next?" I asked, my voice trembling.

He locked the door behind us, his eyes glittering with longing, with the force of his need. He wanted me – I wanted him – and in that moment I couldn't think, couldn't concentrate on anything but how much I wanted him. He pulled me into the bedroom, pressing his lips on mine, his body against mine so tight that I could feel just how much he wanted me, just how much I wanted him...his kisses were hungry, desperate; my hands slid into his hair, gripping at him as I pulled him closer to me. I had wanted this for so long – wanted to kiss him, to run my hands up and down his tantalizingly chiseled chest.

Forget the damn rules, I thought to myself. *Technically, this isn't dating...we've never been on a date.*

Then his top was on the floor – he was lifting my blouse over my head, kissing my breasts, pushing me back on the bed as I shuddered with pleasure, his mouth trailing from my navel to the top of my thigh. "You're more beautiful than I imagined," he groaned. "But I wonder...how do you taste..."

The rational part of my brain told me I should hold back, figure out what was going on, clarify expectations, or just bloody *run away* before things got messy.

I told the rational part of my brain to shut the hell up.

"Chemistry, huh?" was all I could say.

"I told you...we had to resolve it, one way or the other." He murmured against my neck. "Get it out of the way. For the band, remember?" he teased.

"Well, if it's for the band..."

"Neither one of us can go another second being tortured like this – I can feel it, you can feel it. If we're going to play together, we've got to get this desire out of our systems, this second..."

"Right this second." His skin tasted sweet and salty, tantalizing me as I nibbled his chest and shoulders, making my way hungrily to his lips.

Just as his fingers were fumbling with my jeans zipper, I heard the phone ring.

"Damn..." I muttered, silencing it. But it kept on vibrating – the caller calling back again and again.

"Oh, who *is* that?" Danny groaned, frustrated. "Just turn it off."

I looked down in horror as I saw the caller ID. The one name you least want to see when you're about to have wild sex with the guy you've been fantasizing about every day.

"It's my dad."

Chapter 12

Oh, shit. My face was bright scarlet, a combination of pulsing desire and absolute humiliation. Just as I was about to get busy with Danny Blue – making all of my erotic dreams come true at once – I was interrupted by the single worst possible intrusion: my dad on the caller ID. I was pretty sure he'd seen the pictures of me playing at the gig – and with it, figured out that I was a rocker just like dear old dad, bound to end up on that same track which my father was utterly convinced could only lead inexorably to lots of sex, lots of drugs, and plenty of diseases. The second two I minded – at this second, I couldn't imagine that the first would bother me too much. Still, I had to get home right away, to deal with this crisis before my father personally had me and the rest of the Never Knights banned from every reputable club in the country. And knowing my father, that wouldn't be difficult. Even if he wasn't a rock star – he knew enough to threaten the club for having allowed four under-twenty-ones unlimited access to their "champagne suites" and bottle service – and to threaten to make enough of a fuss to get their license revoked. I grimaced. I could only imagine what a mess this conversation with my dad was going to turn out to be.

Danny had evidently picked up on my distress. He came over to me, wrapping his arms around my stomach as he pulled me to his naked chest, his waist tight against me, his hard-on deliriously, tantalizingly pressed against my back. He nibbled lightly on my earlobes, his fingers lightly stroking my nipples where they escaped from the delicate lace of my bra. I closed my eyes in sheer pleasure as his fingers relentlessly flicked back and forth, making it hard for me to concentrate. For a second my body relaxed, instinctively forgetting all my tension and all my worry as I gave myself over to the warm pleasure of his touch. "What's the matter, darling?" he asked, his hot breath ever so slightly tickling my ear, his tongue flecking against my earlobe.

"I've got to...Danny..." I pleaded half-heartedly, but he wasn't having any of it. No sooner had I put on an item of clothing – a sock, a shoe, my jeans – than he took it off, taking advantage of an unprotected area to teasingly slip the clothing from my body. I tried to concentrate, but I couldn't bring myself to push him away, let alone to leave.

I'd never felt like this before. This overwhelming sense of desire that clouded my brain and made me want to vanish into his arms, give myself over to the wealth of physical sensation. I couldn't breathe; I couldn't think. In a matter of days my life had gone from my number-one project, the thing I worked hard to control, to spiraling into utter chaos. Ever since Danny Blue had come into my life, I couldn't do anything but give myself over to the passion I felt for him.

"He's going to be so pissed at me..." I murmured. "I've got to go..."

"Really..." Danny flicked my navel with his tongue. "You have to go *right now*?" His smile was so filled with longing, so filled with ideas of exactly what he'd like to do to me, that I couldn't help but lean back onto the pillow, allowing him to take off my bra, my jeans, everything but my underwear, which he kissed lightly – maddeningly – before looking back up at me.

"Whatever..." I sighed. "I can't control what he thinks, what the public thinks, what that stupid stalker John Flint thinks, what anyone thinks...they're going to say whatever they want to say."

"Exactly," said Danny, still kissing me. "You can't control what other people think about you Neve. You can only control yourself."

If only I could control myself.

"You can't handle everything on your own, Neve. So why don't you let go, okay?" He smiled, his eyes glittering with desire. "Let go." He slid his hand into my underwear, stroking the lace, his hands just close enough to make me release a slight gasp. "Why don't you relax and let me...handle things for a while, okay"

"But my dad..." I half-protested.

"Are you really thinking about your *dad* at a time like this?" he gave a low laugh before stopping, withdrawing his hand and instead wrapping his fingers around mine. "Look, Neve – if you really want me to stop, I'm happy to. Well, not happy, but...I want to do what feels good. For you. For both of us. But if you just need to relax, to de-stress...I'm here to help you do that." He smiled a slow sexy, smile. "I'll take pleasure in making you forget about everything, Neve. Trust me, I'm very good at lovemaking. Whatever you have to deal with tomorrow, you can deal with tomorrow. Let your dad have some time to cool off, to think things over. And you – I want to bring you pleasure more than you know. I've been dreaming about this, about how you would look when you finally lose control. I promise – you'll have a clearer mind in the morning. We both will..."

I looked at him, frozen by his expression. My eyes stared into his. And then, before I knew what I was doing, I nodded...

"Good," he whispered, kissing my lips, his tongue slightly touching the corner of my lips, pressing the length of his body against mine. I could feel the full throbbing force of his desire, feel that unfamiliar but thrilling hardness against my thigh as he wrapped his ankles around mine. I couldn't believe it. It still felt strange – like a dream. He wanted me. Danny Blue, the sexiest, most sophisticated, most worldly guy I'd ever met, wanted me. He wanted me as badly as I wanted him.

"How about I take care of you tonight, Neve? You had a rough night, didn't you? I get that. So why don't we focus on you first...and worry about the other stuff later..." He laughed softly. "I always said music was one of the things I loved doing most in the world. And that's still true. But there's something else that comes *awfully* close..." He grinned as his fingers caressed the inside of my thighs, making me shudder, tracing a slow and inexorable path upwards that made me moan slightly, my lips meeting the edge of his left palm, which still rested against my cheek. "I know you're a control freak, Neve. I can recognize the type. But that's exactly the type I love to watch lose control. The kind who would enjoy it most. I can tell. You'll enjoy this."

I already am.

But something held me back. Whatever happened tonight – it would be the first time for me. I wasn't a stranger to the facts of life – growing up with Keith Knight, half of whose lyrics contained explicit references to several sex acts, taught me all I needed to know. I'd certainly been no stranger to my own fantasies – more than a few of them in recent days about Danny Blue. But there was a difference between theory and practice, as my guitar teacher always used to say – and a difference that what was about to happen was set to make frighteningly clear.

"Wait, Danny..." I said. "Hold up. There's something you should know..."

"Yeah?" He smiled at me.

"This is – well, don't freak out, okay?"

"Okay..." He raised an eyebrow. "What, are you going to tell me you've got some incriminating tattoo."

"I'm a..." *Spit it out, girl.* I wasn't ashamed, after all. Or was I? "This is my first time, okay?"

Danny's mouth fell open. "No!"

"Sorry?"

"Sorry?" He laughed. "No – I'm sorry – I mean, it's nothing to apologize for. I just figured – you know, given how much sex the rest of your band members seem to be having, surrounded by adoring groupies..."

I shook my head. "I've just – I mean, I'm not really interested in too many people. The guys in the band are like brothers to me – and I don't have time to meet too many others." I racked my brains, trying to think what Patti Smith or Siouxsie Sioux would say in a situation like this. "I'm still – you know, if you're still up for it..." I sat up. "I waited because I wanted to wait for someone I'd enjoy it with. And I think – if you're cool – I'd enjoy it a lot with you."

Danny grinned. "I certainly hope so."

"So, you don't have to worry – you don't have to hold back."

He leaned in and kissed me again. "It just means I'll have to work extra hard," he said. "To make this special. For both of us. Not that you weren't already extra special to me, love. I'll go slowly, okay? And be as gentle as you want..."

"You don't have to be gentle," I said quickly. I'd imagined this moment plenty of times in my fantasies, never dreaming it would be real. But if I was going to lose my virginity to Danny Blue, I knew exactly how I wanted it to be. And the words "slow" and "gentle" didn't factor into the equation.

"I like a girl who knows what she wants," he kissed my ear.

"I like a guy who can give it to me."

"Then why don't you lie back, love," his voice teased me into submission. "And let me *give it to you*."

"You can handle me however you like, only..." I looked up at him. "I don't have any condoms."

If his face fell, it was only for a moment. But Danny was too smooth to let that distract him. "Don't worry," he said. "We'll just focus on you tonight, then. There's a time and a place for everything, and under...shall we say, more auspicious circumstances, I'd hold off on *that* particular pleasure until you beg me to do otherwise. As for tonight, there's a whole lot else we can do..."

He smiled wickedly before pulling my panties down, his tongue lightly flicking at my inner thigh, tracing a spiral that got closer – ever-closer – to where his fingers were already lightly stroking. He turned his head slightly – just slightly – the angle between his lips and my thighs just right...

When his moist tongue reached me, I nearly jumped out of my skin. I felt myself moan aloud.

"Don't stop."

His laugh rippled through my whole body, the deep rumble of it coursing through his chest and vibrating through to my sensitive skin. Even that was pleasurable.

"Who said anything about *stopping,* love? We've only just begun..."

Chapter 13

I woke up completely naked, wrapped in Danny's arms for the second morning in a row. Who could have imagined that, twenty-four hours ago, when I was rushing out of Danny's bedroom, that we'd end the night like this? It felt so good to be close to him, utterly naked – and from what I could feel beneath the covers, leaning against my stomach, he was as naked as I was.

"Good morning..." Danny was leaning on the pillow, smiling over at me. "Sleep well, love?" He pulled me close to him, his mouth meeting mine in a kiss at once savage and playful.

There was something so strange, so surreal about this – and yet at the same time so completely natural. It was as if I'd always been meant to wake up in the morning in Danny Blue's arms, and this was just the first time I'd been able to do so.

"Good morning," I murmured back, matching his smile with one of my own. I relaxed into his hard, firm body.

"How are you feeling?" Danny asked me, stroking my collarbone with his velvety fingertips. "Of course, I can only imagine..." He reached playfully under the covers, his fingers finding just what they were looking for.

"Good," I murmured, my body resisting the urge to tense up once again. "Very good indeed."

"I'm glad," he said. "Because I've got to confess, love, I'm awfully keen on doing it again." He flushed slightly. "Last night, when we were in the elevator – I didn't know what this was going to be. A one-time thing, I thought. To get it out of our systems. Once we acted on it, I thought maybe this need..." He pressed closer against me, his need clearly not sated by the previous night, "would go away. But it's stronger than ever, Neve. I think we might need another try to get this out of our systems once and for all." He laughed softly. "Or maybe two. Or three..." He leaned over and pressed his lips against my hair. "You're like a drug, Neve. I'm utterly insatiable when it comes to you."

I looked at him, flushing with delight. I too hadn't been sure what Danny wanted – what *I* wanted – we'd been so caught up in the heat of the moment that neither one of us had talked about it. But from the hours of pleasure he'd given me last night, I knew now that I was eager to explore things further – to see just how far to the brink he could push me before I'd lose control completely. How liberating it was for me to lose control with Danny. But now it seemed Danny was ready to come back for me.

"Already?" I teased. "I thought you'd be exhausted. I mean – all that work you did last night..." I stretched out on the bed. "I'm talking, of course, about your work on the guitar..."

"Oh, really?" he took me into his arms. "That's what you were talking about, huh?"

"All those amazing things you did with your fingers...you know, those guitar solos..."

"Oh, those guitar solos, of course..."

"And with your tongue."

"You mean my vocals."

"That's *exactly* what I mean..." I pressed my lips against his. "Mostly."

"Mostly."

"Hold on a second, love..." He kissed me on the shoulder and got up, going over to where he'd left his bag. Watching his naked body cross the room filled me with a new shuddering wave of desire. His body was utterly perfect. Toned, tanned a smooth golden brown, his buttocks firm and tight – I wanted every inch of him against me. And when he turned around...

"Enjoying the show?" he laughed, turning to face me, fully naked.

"Oh, I'm impressed." I lived in a house with a pool and a steam room – I was no stranger to the male member. I'd even walked in on Kyle once or twice in the locker rooms – both of us crimson and laughing off the embarrassment. And while Kyle was certainly well-equipped in that department, what Danny had to offer was significantly more impressive. I didn't think it could get to that size.

Danny grinned. "You know what they say, love. It's not about the equipment. It's about the performance."

"Well, I'm happy to give that a test drive..." I pulled him back towards the bed. "I think I definitely owe *you* a few hours of relaxation. And I promise you – I'm a fast learner." *New mental checklist,* I thought to myself. *Buy panties. Condoms. Breath mints.*

"As much as I'd love to continue where we left off last night, my darling – it will have to wait for tonight. I've got work."

"Work?" I looked up, confused. "Professor Poe wants you on a Saturday?"

Shit. Why did I have to bring up that Danny was my TA? If the situation in that class wasn't awkward enough before, it certainly would be now...

"No..." Danny pulled out a fresh T-shirt and jeans from his bag and started dressing. "Actually, I've got a second job."

"Teaching doesn't pay the bills?"

"Not quite..."

My eyes traveled to the expensive black Tumi bag on the floor, surprised. Danny had brought an overnight bag to the performance. But he couldn't have known that we'd be staying over – he couldn't have known about the suites. Where had he been planning to stay?

"It's for my dad," Danny said.

"What does he do?"

Danny sighed. "I guess it's time I told you, Neve. I should have known you'd understand – but when I tell you, I hope you'll understand why I haven't. The same reason you didn't tell me about your father...."

He fixed his clear blue eyes on mine, looking at me intently. "Have you heard of Beyond Blue?"

"Yeah, of course. It's the hottest new club in Vegas. I heard Rihanna was there last week..."

"Beyond Blue. Owned by Clarence Blue."

"Yeah?"

"Well..."

Danny waited for it to hit me. Clarence Blue – the richest mogul in the hospitality industry – bigger than the Hiltons, known for the most exclusive and star-studded nightclubs, hotels, and casinos between here, Palm Beach, London, and Paris, and Bali.

"Your..."

"Dad," Danny finished the sentence for me.

My mouth fell open. If I thought I had a public image to hide as Keith Knight's daughter, Danny had it twentyfold. Clarence Blue wasn't just rich. He was the biggest celebrity of them all – a man who made his name by being flamboyant and over-the-top, a man who frequently had designated Girlfriends One, Two, and Three, who'd been married more times than Zsa Zsa Gabor, who'd had an affair with anyone who'd ever made it on the cover of Rolling Stone...

"This hotel..." Danny said. "I didn't want to say anything. But there's a reason they gave us the nicest suite. And it wasn't just because they felt bad about John Flint."

"You own it?"

"It's one of our smaller properties."

"And that bag?"

"I called them last night – asked them to provide me with this change of clothes. The staff is used to me traveling around from hotel to hotel to check up on them once in a while, especially when my dad's away in London. It's part of the deal I cut to let me go away to California..."

"What do you mean?"

"My doctorate – I do that because I love it. I'm funded – paying for it myself with my teaching. I don't want to live off my father's name, any more than you do. But my dad – he wanted me to go into the hotel business. He agreed to let me go off to California without interfering or objecting. He insisted on giving me money – money I don't need or want. But I agreed on one condition. I'd work for it, like everyone else in his company. He tries to give me the cushiest assignments – but I want to earn my dues." He flushed. "When my dad found out I liked to play, he encouraged it. I think he thinks it will help his image to have a pro rocker for a son. He hired me the best tutors money could buy; he called in favors from everyone from Springsteen to Mick Jagger. And a *lot* of people owed him favors. When I got good, I joined Peyton's band." His eyes darkened at the mention of her name. He sat down alongside me, running his hand up and down my backside, my body crushed against his.

"I would have told you earlier – but I didn't want it to influence you. Either for or against me."

"I understand," I said. "I didn't want to tell you, either."

"We understand each other, then," Danny smiled. "I'm glad. Someone else who gets how crazy this whole life is." He pointed to another bag on the coffee table. "I called this morning before you woke up and had them bring some clothes for you, too. We've got a personal shopper at Neiman's Beverly Hills – I got your size from the labels." His arms encircled my waist. "I'm sure you'd look gorgeous in anything, but you'll like what the staff picked out for you..."

I was overwhelmed. My parents had personal shoppers, of course – as did most of the celebrities in Beverly Hills – but I'd always preferred to lurk incognito in vintage stores, avoiding that world. Now that world was staring me in the face.

"Babe, I'm so sorry to leave like this – but I'll miss my flight if I don't hurry up."

"I have to fly to Chicago today to check on a new property." He kissed me lightly, his teeth smooth against my lips. "But I want to see you tonight, Neve." His voice was husky with desire. "I'm not done with you, yet. Come to my place tonight. I want more of you. A whole lot more." He kissed me thoroughly then.

And I knew that I wanted him too. "Okay," I whispered.

"And bring...whatever you like." He kissed me one more time. "I'll be thinking of you all day."

When he was gone, I sighed with a mixture of exhaustion and relief. Being around him was almost too tiring – my body ached from how tense I'd been all night. I slipped into the turquoise sundress and sandals in the bag, impressed at how well they fit. Danny wanted to spoil me, apparently. I flushed. What I thought was going to be a one-night fling was shaping up to be a lot more than that.

But if this desire I felt was anything to go by, I knew neither of us could ever be satisfied with just one night.

Chapter 14

No sooner had I driven back to the dorm and entered the common room than I felt a mysterious sinking feeling in the pit of my stomach. Everyone was staring at me – people I'd shared bathrooms and corridors with for weeks without so much as giving me a second glance were now looking me up and down like I was a piece of meat. I didn't even have to ask – I knew that they knew. I'd tried to keep my celebrity status quiet – I'd changed my name from the decidedly hippie "Never" to the much more conventional "Neve", and done my best to avoid talking about my family altogether – but now I knew it was too late.

"Hey baby..." A frat guy I recognized as living on my hall approached me, belching out gas that smelled distinctly like beer. *"You make my chest burn, baby – you make me shake, like only you know how..."*

Those were my dad's lyrics. Lyrics I'd grown up with. But in this guy's mouth they sounded filthy, sordid. I flushed scarlet.

"Come on, baby – give us a kiss..." He lumbered forward. "Just like you gave that other guy. Do you do that with all your fans, baby? Just like your dad..."

"Fat chance," I spat, turning crimson as I hurried to my room. My face was scarlet and hot – with shame, with fury. All it had taken was one blog post and my life was turned upside down overnight. When I first arrived at college I'd dreamed of being normal, of blending in, of making friends – of shedding this image of a Beverly Hills party girl that had claimed, one by one, all my friends growing up. But I was a fool. I should have known that my past would come back to haunt me, as it always did. Now that everyone knew who I was, I wasn't safe. The tiniest indiscretion, the silliest drunken moment – anyone who lived at the dorms with me could take a picture and upload it to the internet in no time.

A knock at the door interrupted me.

"Come in..." I muttered. "If you're here to kiss me..."

"I'm not." Kyle looked abashed. "Neve, I heard what happened. I'm sorry I wasn't there." His eyes were so wide and so full of pain I almost wanted to comfort *him*. Poor Kyle – so sweet, so sensitive – had a habit of taking insults to me more personally than I did.

I reached out to hug Kyle. "Nothing to worry about," I sighed. "It was just some stupid kids acting like...well...stupid kids. They're just being immature. Just ignore that."

"I heard that Harry Prescott tried to shove his tongue down your throat." Kyle gritted his teeth. "I always knew he was a jerk. If you want me to hunt him down, Neve, just say the word..."

"Thanks," I sighed. "But no thanks, Kyle. He was just being stupid. I think I'm going to avoid the dorms for a while. I'm thinking about moving out, actually."

Kyle's face fell. He looked crestfallen. "Neve, don't tell me you're giving up? Letting some jerk like Harry Prescott run you off?"

"It's not like that," I said. "It's just – if people know about my dad, I need to be a bit more careful. The paps could get wind of where I am – I don't want pictures of me in the shower ending up on TMZ."

Kyle nodded. "So you're moving back to your parents' place, then?" He gulped. "If you do, you know, I could move back with you. We could commute in together. Your mom would never forgive me if she thought I was abandoning you..."

"I'm too old to run back to Mommy and Daddy like a spoiled baby," I sighed. "I don't want that, either." But as I looked around at my roommate's scattered clothes and obviously unhidden bong, I knew I was just kidding myself. I couldn't be a normal college kid, no matter how much I wanted to be.

"Then what will you do?" Kyle turned to me.

"I was thinking of getting my own place, like Luc and Steve," I mused. "The complex they live in has a couple of apartments free – I saw a "to rent" sign up last time I went over..."

Kyle grinned. "Well, that will be convenient, won't it? Then you guys can all share the commute into town –

and when we practice, you won't have to go far..." He looked up at me. "So, do you need a roommate?"

"Don't be ridiculous, Kyle – you don't have to give up dorm life for me! You're a freshman – go have fun!"

"I'd have more fun with you, Neve," said Kyle. "I love meeting new people, I love the dorms. But I like hanging out with you, more."

I couldn't help thinking about Danny, about last night, about the pleasure I'd experienced, about the way we hadn't had to worry about keeping quiet – the way I'd moaned aloud.

"I was thinking of getting a place by myself, actually," I said. "As much as I love hanging out with you, I don't think we'd make the best roommates..."

"What are you talking about?" Kyle said. "We'd make great roommates. All through when we were kids we slept near each other, spent all our time together. Pretended to go camping in your bedroom and set up a tent on your floor. Plus, I'm convinced your mother doesn't trust anyone but me to take care of you..."

I felt a pang of guilt. Kyle and I had always been close – after what had happened to his mother and father he'd clung to me and to my family as the only semblance of normalcy he had left – but sometimes his sensitivity, his need to be close to me, felt a bit overwhelming.

"Kyle, I kind of want to be on my own for a bit."

"But we've never lived apart before..." Kyle protested. "Not ever! You're my best friend. When I first moved here..." I knew the story. I remembered the pale, tragic-faced boy he had once been – the boy who had watched his father shoot his mother right in front of him. A boy whose bruises had not yet healed when he moved in. "You took care of me. When I had no friends, no confidence, nothing..."

"But you have all those things now, Kyle. You don't need me."

"We could get a two-bedroom. Then we'd have our own space." He leaned in close to me – *really* close, I noted. Close enough that his lips were but inches from my own. "I'll make sure the paps stay away – I'll take care of that for you. I'll take care of everything." He leaned in softly, pressing his lips against my cheek. "At least, if you go away, promise me one thing. You'll let Luc and Steve keep an eye on you – make sure nothing like what happened the other night happens again."

"I'm Keith Knight's daughter, not the President's daughter," I said. "I don't need the Secret Service watching me. What's the worst that can happen?"

"I just don't want that thing with John Flint happening again. I don't want anyone touching my girl."

His voice was strangely intense, possessive in a way that frightened me. I tried to laugh it off. "Don't worry, I can defend myself against the creeps."

But Kyle did not smile. "I mean – I don't want *anyone* touching you like that..." He flushed scarlet. I'd always suspected Kyle had feelings for me – we were both hormonal teenagers together, after all – but I'd figured they'd worn off with time. I'd always known he was attached to me. Too attached, maybe, but with the childhood he'd had who could blame him? He was used to losing the people he loved.

"I'll keep my cell phone on, all the time, in case you need to reach me."

He leaned in and for a terrifying moment I thought he was going to kiss me. But instead he just lightly brushed his lips against my cheek.

"Neve, you don't get it, do you? Whatever happens after the shows, with girls, with whoever – you're the one that matters to me. You're the only important person in my life, well, you and Aunt Tamara. You were always there for me. When I wanted to go visit my dad in jail, and Auntie T wouldn't let me. When I ran away..."

"I knew you'd come back."

"You sat in the back of your dad's car for days, making the chauffeur drive in circles around LA until they found me."

"I remember..." I smiled, but his words were breaking my heart. "You sure know how to hide, don't you? When you want to be left alone. You had me so worried, then..."

"You know why I came back, though?"

I had a feeling, but I couldn't bring myself to do more than nod.

"Kyle..."

"Because of you, Neve. So I could see you again."

I didn't want to talk about this – I couldn't bear to talk about this. *No dating in the band* – that was the rule. My rule. A rule I'd already broken once today.

"If we can't be roommates, if we can't be close..."

"Kyle, I want my privacy."

"Privacy?" Kyle's eyes narrowed. "What do you need privacy for – from me?"

"Because I'm an adult, Kyle! Because we're too old to take baths together and sleep in the same bed like we did when we were little. We're grown up now, both of us – and we're too old to do what we used to do."

Kyle was getting the picture – realizing, at last, too late, that I was pushing him away.

"Of course..." He forced himself to laugh. "I just forget you're a girl sometimes, you know? I'm so used to being around you, I forget it's a bit weird. You're not just a girl; you're my best friend."

"I know, Kyle..." I pulled him close to me in a hug, knowing how much more he wanted from me, knowing I could never give him that...

"Anyway – new topic..." Kyle laughed. "I'm loving the hair. What is that – post-fling chic?"

"What?"

"Please, Neve. Nobody saw you after the show and your hair looks completely wild. And you've got that *glow.*"

"What glow?"

"You know. The glow that means you've just..."

"I have *not!*"

Kyle laughed. "Trust me, Neve. I've been with a lot of girls. I know that glow. You get with a fan?"

"I'm not talking about it."

"Well, that explains your need for privacy, huh? The spoils of being a rock star – just like one of the boys..."

I knew he was only talking like this to dull the pain of my rejection – if I was going to reject him, better to believe that it was because I wanted meaningless sex like the rest of the guys in the band. Better to believe that I was getting it on with groupies. I sighed. Kyle could never know the truth – it would destroy him.

"Kyle, I've got to head home. I need to talk to my dad. He's probably so worried after what happened."

"Let me drive you back," Kyle said. "I need to go home and do some laundry, anyway. I'll be there for you. For moral support."

First Kyle, then my father. This was shaping up to be one stressful day.

Chapter 15

Luckily, my parents weren't home. Mrs. Jostens
greeted me with a smile and an offer of some mid-morning
bacon, but I wasn't up to it. I wanted to be alone with my
thoughts. I went into my room, closing the door behind me.
I felt very old all of a sudden. Kyle was my best friend, my
childhood companion – but he'd always been like a brother
to me. I'd taken him in – or my family had – and he'd
become more than just our housekeeper's nephew. He'd
become one of us. My dad had gotten him guitar lessons
when he got me mine – he ate at the dinner table with us.
He was the brother I'd never had.

I'd always known Kyle had issues with
abandonment – who wouldn't, in his shoes? But I'd never
realized the depth of his feelings for me. Feelings I'd have
to learn to ignore if I wanted to keep the band together.

"Knock knock," Kyle entered the room, sitting next
to me on the bed. He'd done it a hundred times before –
we'd always spent hours lying on this bed together, just
talking. But this time it felt weird – felt different.

"I always thought it would be like this forever," said
Kyle, looking up at the ceiling. "You and me in this room.
A happy family."

"It was nice," I said.

"I don't want to pull a Geoff, Neve. I don't want to make you uncomfortable. But I think...I think I've made my feelings for you quite clear, whether I wanted to or not. And I want you to know I'm not going to act on anything you don't want me to. But – if you ever want me to...I'll be there. Anytime. Anywhere." His lower lip trembled. "I'm crazy about you, Neve Knight. And I just thought you should know." Before I could respond he turned on his heel and walked out, leaving me utterly exhausted and confused. In a few short weeks, I'd had to deal with Geoff, Danny, and now Kyle. *Is it something in the water?* I sighed. Kyle's jealousy made me resolve even harder to keep my relationship with Danny a secret.

But not even my worry could stop me from driving over to Danny's that night. He answered the doorbell with a smile, wearing the same clothes he'd worn that morning.

"I'm afraid I'm simply covered in sweat," he said. "I've only just come back from the airport. I had to go get groceries..."

"Groceries?" I looked up at him. "Are we cooking?"

"Not exactly." Danny smiled. "I had a lot of time in airport lounges today. A lot of time to think. To think about what exactly we could do, you and I." He slipped off my jacket, and I shuddered with pleasure at the sensation of his hands around my shoulders. He kissed me hungrily, devouring me with his embrace. "All I could think about was how beautiful you looked last night. How you smelled.

How gorgeous your face is when you're in the throes of ecstasy – how much you were enjoying it..."

"You think that's beautiful?"

"I think that's mind-bendingly sexy. You're already so beautiful. But when you're....lost in pleasure – your face takes on a whole new character." He kissed me again. "I can't wait to see that expression again. Have you eaten?"

"No..."

"Good..." Danny put a bag of groceries down on the kitchen counter, taking out a box full of strawberries and a chilled bottle of champagne. "We're going to get through all of these tonight..." He looked me up and down. "Only – I haven't got any plates."

He slipped the dress off my body. "Lie down, love." He brought the champagne and the strawberries over.

I lay back, my whole body tingling with pleasure and anticipation.

"What are you doing?"

"I've been fantasizing about doing this to you all day."

He poured the tiniest bit of champagne onto my navel, causing me to moan aloud as the cool liquid fizzed on my belly. He pressed his lips to my stomach and hungrily licked up the champagne, his hot mouth contrasting with the cool liquid.

I gave myself over to pleasure – to the extraordinary sensations of his mouth and tongue and fingers once again working their magic on me. I couldn't bear it – the pleasure was too strong, too overwhelming. I felt like I was drowning in ecstasy, unable to hold back my cries.

He lifted his head slightly. "You don't have to be quiet," he said. "Like I said – there's nobody around to hear the noise. Just let go, Neve…"

Afterward we were both soaked in sweat, the sheets smelling of champagne and of each other.

"So, Mr. Blue," I laughed. "Are we going to keep seeing each other like this?"

"I want to, Neve," Danny kissed me, holding me close. "I want to so much. I still want more of you. A whole lot more."

I snuggled in his arms, pressing a kiss on his chest. "We can't tell anyone, though, Danny. I don't want this getting in the way of the band – the others finding out."

"I understand," said Danny. "I get the feeling that if they find out, it won't be pretty."

"So you know…"

"The guys are possessive of you," Danny said. "Some of them, like Steve, just see you as a kid sister. But others – they care about you. They want to protect you. But it's more than that....you're special to them. And if they know about us…"

"They *can't*," I repeated, thinking of Kyle. Of how much it would hurt him. "I love them all – but they can't know…"

"Especially with class," Danny said. "I can get out of grading your work directly because I'm in the band, and I can declare a conflict of interest. But I don't want to....make any more than that public. I value my reputation, too."

"This is dangerous, Danny," I said.

"Too dangerous?"

"It should be," I said. "Logically, we should just leave each other alone – back off..."

"And are you feeling logical right now..." He traced his fingers up and down my stomach, letting them rest between my legs before beginning slowly, tantalizingly, to explore further...

"No..." I breathed, before leaning back, giving myself over to his nimble touch once more, and to the ecstasy that followed...

Chapter 16

The next few days were the most exquisite kind of torture. Between class and practices, I saw Danny almost constantly. But seeing him in public meant that I couldn't do what I wanted to do – couldn't throw myself before him and give myself over to the force of my desire at every single opportunity. As much as I wanted him, longed for him, craved him – we had to keep at a distance from one another, reducing our relationship to secret smiles, to light stolen touches on the hand, to secret kisses in the corridor while the other band members were practicing. Being so close to one another, staring at each other with an intensity that made it clear we each knew what the other was thinking, that we remembered precisely what we'd gotten up to the night before, made it even harder for me to concentrate. Every night when the band left Danny's, I'd get in my car, circle around the house, and drive back once the others had gone. Each night we got more inventive; things got more exciting. Little by little Danny initiated me into the myriad ways of pleasure – showing me not only how to receive ecstasy but also how to give it. I didn't know what I was doing, at first – but my instincts - and Danny's guiding hand – were good teachers, and soon I found that pleasure came not only from allowing Danny to take control of my body, but also from learning how to take control of his. Each encounter we tried something new – new positions, new words, new alignments of our bodies such that our pleasure increased tenfold every time we experimented. It felt like our bodies had been made for one another. We were wholly consumed with each other. Each time we met, I wanted more and more of him.

And whenever he was gone – whenever he had to take off to Chicago or San Francisco or New York for a few days to check out properties for his dad – I felt it. I felt the strange pain of absence – pain that melded with frustration and made me irritable and snappish. I'd never noticed that this part of my life – sexual fulfillment – was missing for so many years; now that I knew what it was, one day without the mind-blowing orgasms to which I'd become accustomed was enough to drive me to distraction. *Is this what addiction is?* I wondered. *When your body craves something so much – when you feel like you can't live without it....*

A couple of weeks after our last show, Danny was away in New York. I tried to use the time apart productively – the super of Steve and Luc's apartment complex had called me to let me know a studio had become available upstairs from them, and the boys helped me move into the tidy, compact apartment that I was looking forward to calling him. Still, despite the pizzas and the shared banter, the joking and talking that was just like old times, I couldn't help but feel like something was *missing*. Danny's absence was a palpable shadow on the proceedings. I tried to ignore it. All of us – except from Kyle, who still seemed vaguely hurt that I'd turned down his offer to be roommates – were happy, enjoying just hanging out and being together like old times. And then the phone rang.

"Hello?"

It was our booking agent.

"What does she say?" Luc was whispering, as Steve shushed him.

"Listen – The Cure's reunion tour – their opening act just had to cancel. Lead singer got bronchitis. You know what I'm talking about."

"At the Palladium..." My mouth fell open. The Palladium was the biggest, most prestigious amphitheater in LA. "Us?"

"The PALLADIUM?" Kyle almost fell off his chair.

"But listen – it's for tomorrow night. Can you do tomorrow"

"Tomorrow?" I repeated blankly.

"Tomorrow – at the Palladium?" Kyle's eyes widened.

"No way!" Luc exclaimed.

"Of course we can do it," I said automatically, bidding her farewell and hanging up the phone. "Tomorrow. At the Palladium. Opening for The Cure."

The excitement was overwhelming. We were shouting and screaming and falling into one another's arms – overwhelmed at the good news.

"I have to call Danny and tell him!" I said. "He should be heading back soon..." *You think? You've been counting the hours...*

"We'd better get practicing this second," said Steve. "I'd better head downstairs and get us some equipment right away. Neve, we need to practice for the next twenty-four hours straight if we want a shot at playing the Palladium." He laughed, his face flushing with excitement. "I mean – the Palladium. This is the biggest deal ever. We're going to have to play every song through at least three or four times. The opening for The Cure..."

"I know!" I'd never seen Steve this excited. "Wait – where are we practicing?"

"At Danny's..."

"We can't!" I said. "Not yet, I mean. He's just gotten back from New York – he's probably not home for another couple of hours." I picked up the phone. No sooner had Danny answered than I felt my whole body tingling.

"Hey, Gorgeous. Have I been thinking about what I want to..."

"I'm with the band," I said loudly, hoping nobody heard his salacious opening.

"Oh," Danny sounded disappointed. "How are the guys?"

When I told him the news, I could practically hear his grin over the telephone. "No way," he said. "I knew you could do it, babe. I've got a layover in Chicago – I'm there now. Should be home in three hours flat. I'll put my pedal on the gas just for you."

After I hung up and told the guys the news, they cheered.

"But what do we do in the meanwhile?" Luc asked.

I smiled a mischievous smile. "We celebrate," I said. "Like true rock stars. By breaking the rules."

"What do you mean...?"

"I'm new," I said. "I don't know the rules here. *Are* there any music rules? I don't think there are. I think we can jam as loud as we want..."

Steve, Luc, and Kyle broke into matching grins. "What the heck? Why not?"

Steve and Kyle went downstairs to bring up the equipment, leaving me alone with Luc. He smiled softly, chuckling to himself.

"What is it?" I asked him.

"Who'd have thought it – so many years ago? That we'd end up like this..." Luc turned to me. "We're really doing it, Neve. All of us – growing up. And *you...*" he turned to look at me, melting me with his chocolate-brown eyes. "You've grown up most of all." He took a step towards me. "Oh, Neve – today, apparently, dreams are coming true for us. Let's see how many come true..." He touched my cheek lightly. "I'm so glad you're moving close to me..."

"You're always welcome to come over. We can..."

But before I could finish my sentence, Luc's lips were on mine; he was pulling me towards him, kissing me passionately, his whole body taut with desire. I was shocked – overwhelmed. *Luc*? Luc didn't like me like that – Luc and I were just...but the force of his kiss knocked all thought right out of me.

"Luc..." I pulled away, trying to regain my balance, not to mention my sanity. "Luc, I can't..."

But a loud, angry cough caused us both to turn our heads toward the door. "So it's Luc, is it?" Kyle looked furious. "He's the one you've been seeing behind our backs?" He marched in, his face red with anger. "He's the reason you haven't been in your dorm room ten nights this term..."

I felt anger rise in my chest. How *dare* Kyle attempt to keep track of me, try to tell me who I could and couldn't see, what I could or couldn't do? All sympathy I had for his unrequited crush vanished. "What, are you keeping track of me like some crazed stalker or something?"

"It's my *job* to keep an eye on you, Neve. What if John Flint or someone came back."

"It's not your *job* to do anything!" I shouted.

"Well, I was worried about you, that's all." He sneered. "But now I see I don't have to worry. It was Luc all along. So much for all your *rules*, huh? No dating anyone in the band? Or I guess that just applied to me..."

"Look..." Even now Luc was calm, collected. Mature. "I have no idea what you're talking about, Kyle. Neve has never spent the night with me. Ask Steve – he'd know!"

Kyle took a step towards Luc, getting straight into his face. "Don't deny it, man. I've always known – you think you're so clever, hiding it? But I see the way you look at her, man. I know you wanted her. I thought we were friends, yeah? I thought you'd never go for her behind my back, knowing how I..."

"How dare you!" I wanted to slap Kyle clean across the face.

"I would *never*," Luc said, looking as angry as I felt. "Even if...even if I *did* have feelings for Neve – which I'm not saying I do..." his face turned cherry-red. "But if I *did*...I wouldn't break the rules, okay? I know the rules – same as anyone else. I just got...I was excited, okay? About the gig. I just needed to blow off some steam."

My heart sank. I'd always known that this was going to happen, that my great fear would be realized. My love life would drive a wedge between me and the band.

"Is that what you call it? When you were shoving your tongue down her throat? Just letting off steam? Don't you respect her?"

"What?" Luc and I said simultaneously.

"She's not some groupie you can just mess with and then leave behind..."

"I don't think *anyone* is someone you can just mess with and leave behind, Kyle," said Luc in a warning tone of voice. "And if Neve wanted to sleep with someone – me or anyone else for that matter, it's absolutely not your business. You pretend you're her personal bodyguard – pretend her parents are worried about her. But it's you that's worried. You just want to keep track of everything that's going on – who she's with, what's happening. We've all ignored it. But it's creepy, man. And you need to back off, now. Whatever's happening with me and Neve is none of your concern."

"Nothing *is* happening." My high-pitched voice stopped them just short of coming to blows. "Between me and Luc."

"Who, then?" Kyle turned on me. "Clearly you're getting it from *somewhere*. It's obvious. The way you just walk around..."

"You want to talk about my *glow*?" I snapped. "It's none of your business where I'm getting it from. Or whom. It's my business."

"Is that true..." Luc looked at me, shock spreading over his face. "Are you seeing someone?"

I sighed. I hadn't wanted my love life to get between me and the band – and now it would have to. I nodded. "I mean no. I mean yes. I mean – it's not serious, not yet, anyway. It's just....you know, casual sex. Not a *thing*." Was I telling the truth? I wasn't sure. Whatever Danny and I had, it wasn't meaningless. But we definitely weren't an "item," either.

Luc sighed. "Neve...I thought you had more sense than that!"

This made me angry. Luc – who went out with a different girl every night – had the nerve to lecture *me* on my choices! "And *you* stay home and drink water after every gig?" I snapped. "Why is it different for you than it is for me, huh? You have more casual sex than anyone I know. You do *not* get to judge me..."

"It's not like that..." Luc shook his head, trying to explain. "It's just – you're *Neve*. You're like a sister to me."

"Not *that* like a sister," Kyle cut in loudly.

"I just don't want to see you get hurt by the guys who are looking for casual flings..."

"Guys like you, you mean?"

That shut him up.

"Nobody should just want you for that. I mean – you're the kind of girl a guy could proudly bring home to his family. The girl I could always bring home to my mom."

"I still am."

"No guy should just want you for sex, that's all I'm saying. You could do better."

I couldn't help baiting him. "And what if I just want *him* for sex? What – am I damaged goods, now? I'm not a virgin – so suddenly you can't take me home to Mommy? Please – so I'm having sex with my boyfriend. You want to judge? Judge Kyle – who takes home a different girl every night. Maybe you can't take *him* to your mother's house, either! *He's* not a virgin. And neither are you, Luc. Guys and their double standards."

"So he's your boyfriend?" Luc's eyes widened with pain.

"And *unlike* you guys, the guy I'm seeing – incidentally – hasn't been with a different girl every night for the past year. I know where he's been. We're monogamous. And it's safe."

Seeing Luc and Kyle's stricken expressions, I felt a bit ashamed of my outburst. I was right, I felt, to defend myself – both Luc and Kyle were holding me to an unfair double standard, and they knew it. But I knew too the real reasons for their reaction – the jealousy that made both of them say such ugly things. "Don't worry," I said. "Like I said, it's casual. My priority is on the band. The band comes first."

Chapter 17

We spent the rest of that day practicing – once Steve came and the tension dissipated, we tried to ignore the fight we'd had. Luc and Kyle were still awkward around each other – and I was still fuming. I liked my friends – loved them, even. Certainly I respected them. But for the first time I realized what a difference a few years made in our relationship. Suddenly the fact of my being a woman was a *big deal* in the way it had never been when we were kids. Sure, I was flattered that Luc saw me as a "good girl," "girlfriend material," - someone superior to the groupies he slept with. But more than that, I was disturbed by what it said about Luc – that he was perfectly willing to sleep with girls *he* didn't consider "girlfriend material" precisely *because* they were willing to sleep with him, and to judge them for it. I almost felt sorry for his groupies, for Kyle's. A lot of them, I imagined, were girls just like me – girls happy to be driven for the moment by desire. And if Danny hadn't lost respect for me for agreeing to our relationship – a relationship that was driven in part by lust – then why should anyone else?

Maybe my dad was right to try to shield me from this world, I thought bitterly. Maybe being a woman in a group of rock stars wasn't all it's cracked up to be. Still, I tried to ignore my annoyance and focus on the work at hand. Kyle and Luc were still boys, after all – still teenagers at eighteen and nineteen. *Danny would never treat me this way.* He didn't think I was anything but a "good girl" - even when I was naked and writhing on his bed in ecstasy. He *loved* the pleasure we shared – the trust that had made us both capable of learning to articulate what we wanted without flushing, to share our fantasies, to trust each other with our whole bodies.

The tension in the air was still palpable at the end of the rehearsal. Steve came up to me, lightly tapping me on the shoulder. "What's going on?" Steve asked me.

"Nothing," I shrugged him away. "Nothing I want to talk about."

"Fine," said Steve, to my relief. At least Steve had managed to get through this semester without going as crazy as the rest of us. "Let's skip Danny's solo and go straight to the bridge..."

Kyle and Luc were still glowering at one another.

"Come on guys," I said, rolling my eyes. "Can't we be grown-ups here for the night? We only have tonight to practice..."

"Fine," said Luc. "Just for the night."

Just for the night? My heart sank. Did Luc mean to quit the band?

"Luc," my voice softened. "I'm sorry – I really am. I know – we've got a lot to talk about, okay? And we will talk about it. Just not tonight. We'll talk after the show. I'm sorry I didn't tell you I was seeing someone – I only told Kyle, because it was new and I didn't think it was important..."

He nodded glumly. "Whoever you're with," he murmured, "is one lucky son of a bitch." His eyes did not meet my own.

"Kyle, you okay?"

"Fine," Kyle said glumly. "I've got a guitar in my hands already, don't I? I'm ready. So let's get this over with."

We were interrupted by a knock at the door. My heart leaped. Was it Danny? But to my disappointment it was just the super, looking beleaguered and exhausted.

"You guys know the noise rules..." he said. "Really, you know that..."

"She won't have to worry about that." Danny's familiar, velvety voice made my heart jump. "Where she's going, she can make all the noise she likes." He smiled at me as he emerged in the doorway, his black jeans and t-shirt stretched across his broad shoulders and hard abs leaving little to my imagination. Even after three hours of travel Danny looked every inch the rock star. The super, clearly recognizing in Danny some easy authority, grumbled a bit about the neighbors before departing.

I walked out into the corridor to bid farewell to the super. But before I could re-enter my apartment Danny pulled me into an alcove, kissing me hungrily. "Neve," he murmured. "I've missed you so much."

"I've missed you too." Already I could feel my whole body reacting to his, eager for his touch. I wanted to kiss him for hours, but I didn't want to rouse suspicions. "Listen," I said. "Play it cool tonight. Kyle and Luc got into blows over me – they know I'm seeing someone but don't know who...Kyle thought it was Luc..."

Danny bit his lip, anger flashing briefly over his face. "I see – so, Luc made a pass at you?"

"Not a pass," I said quickly. "It was very innocent. Kyle just misinterpreted things..."

"Good," said Danny firmly. "Because there's nothing innocent about what I've got planned for you tonight. I'll play it cool tonight, Neve – but stay over tonight, okay? I want to show you how much I missed you."

We headed back into the apartment and loaded the instruments into the car before heading to Danny's. We practiced until sunrise, absolutely shattered, until at last we headed back to our cars.

"Want to get dinner?" Kyle asked me. "Or breakfast, really. At this hour."

"Actually, I'm going to..." I sighed. "I'm going to make a detour, get some gas, refuel. You go home without me."

"Are you sure?" Kyle looked disappointed. "I really wanted to talk."

"I'm sure," I said. "I'm tired and I could use a good night's sleep. Or what's left of it."

Kyle's voice sounded strained. "I know," he said, sighing. "I get it. I'll let the others know." He turned to me. "I hope you get whatever you need out of your system," he said. "So you can move on. And realize that there's a lot of guys out there..." his voice choked, "who would give you a lot more than sex. There's a lot of guys who would love to be with you, who would cherish you, who would do anything for you."

"I appreciate that," I said, "But Kyle, I'm not looking for that right now. And even if I were..." *Not with you.* I couldn't bear to say those words out loud to him.

"Right. Goodnight." Kyle turned around and walked to his car. I waited until he was safely gone before heading back inside to Danny's, my body burning with longing.

"I'm back...." I breathed. "I finally got away."

For a moment Danny seemed distracted – his face pale, his eyes distant.

"Danny, are you okay?"

At once he snapped out of it. His face transformed – the look of yearning on his face sending my body into a frenzy. Barely a moment had passed before we had torn each other's jeans off and were lying on the bed.

"It's been three whole days," Danny nuzzled my shoulder. "Did I tell you how much I missed you? I told Steve I was shattered – but truth is I think I can find just a bit more energy left, can't you...?"

He lifted me up, turning me over so that my legs rested on his shoulders, his face facing my bare stomach. "This," he announced slyly, "is but the first course." He began kissing my stomach, his mouth and body shifting so that his tongue trailed further down...

Before long my whole body was shaking with relief.

"Hard day..." he asked, when I was still at last. "I'm exhausted – and now completely sweaty. Why don't you join me in the shower?" he grinned. "I get the sense you could use a relaxing shower too, after the horrid day you've had."

With the water streaming all around us, drowning out the noise, we moved onto other pursuits – he had brought me to the brink of ecstasy seconds earlier, and now it was my turn to do the same, taking hold of him and playing with his body gently before slipping to my knees, anxious to taste every inch of his tan, beautiful body. It seemed that hours passed before Danny wrapped me in a towel and all but carried me to the bed. Utterly spent, we had no more energy for passion. Instead his touch was gentle, delicate. Even romantic. He caressed my cheeks, my shoulders, his eyes wide not with desire but with something else – something more.

"I missed you very much, Danny," I said.

"I know. I missed you too. I wish you could've gone with me. Maybe next time..." he sighed. "Next time you'll come with me. How does that sound?"

"That sounds great."

He nuzzled my ear and I couldn't help but smile. For all Kyle and Luc's judgment, what we had was more than just sex. There was something meaningful there – some connection that I felt more than ever now, when things were so still, when I was lying with my head against his chest...

"So, there will be a next time," I said.

"Of course, Neve..." he said. "You're a part of my life now."

Everything felt so beautiful at that moment, so calm. At that moment, as I drifted off to sleep, resting in the bosom of the man I cared for, I was utterly happy. Dreams slowly took hold of me and I could hear myself muttering, instinctively.

"Night, Danny."

"Night, Neve."

"Love you..."

I hadn't meant to say it – hadn't meant to say anything like that. But no sooner had I spoken than Danny's eyes shot wide open and he sat up on the bed. His whole expression had changed.

"Oh, no..." he muttered. "No, you didn't mean that. You don't mean that."

"I...don't?" I felt my heart sink all at once. Sure it was soon – too soon – but he knew what I meant...

"Neve, I'm sorry." He looked embarrassed now. "I thought we were on the same page about this. That what you wanted – what we both wanted – I'm sorry, I should have realized..."

"Realized what?" my voice was shaking.

"I care for you a lot, Neve. And I'm really enjoying what we have. You're a great friend – and an incredible lover. You're gorgeous and smart and sexy but..."

"But..."

"I thought this was just fun for you. For both of us. No strings – no commitment – that's what we said, right? Neve – you know my story. You know about Peyton. I'm just getting back into things after losing her. A commitment – I mean, if that's what you want, I'm not sure I'm..." He sighed and took my hand, pressing it to his lips. "I'm so sorry, Neve. I thought we wanted the same thing. Great sex, great company, a lot of fun. But I'm not ready to get attached like that again. It's been a year, but sometimes it feels like she only died yesterday." He kissed my forehead. "If you don't want to handle that, if you can't handle that – I understand if you don't want to see me..."

I couldn't listen to another second of this. Every word that Danny spoke was breaking my heart. Before he could open his mouth I was dressed and running out the door, tears streaming down my face, my car heading back towards the only place in the world I felt safe, felt secure, felt insulated from all this chaos.

Back to Mom and Dad.

Chapter 18

It was seven in the morning by the time I arrived home – and all I wanted to do was to lie down and cry on my childhood bed. How could I have been so stupid? Done the one thing I'd told myself I'd never do – fall in love with someone from the band? I had known Danny was older, more sophisticated, more used to "friends with benefits" than I was – I should have known he wouldn't fall in love with me the way I had with him. Maybe Kyle and Luc were right, I thought angrily, I was somebody's fuck-buddy, nothing more.

Just as I thought of him, the phone rang: Kyle was calling. "What?" I was still angry about last night.

"Look, I know you don't want to be disturbed, but Steve and Luc called me to tell me you didn't come back home last night. Are you okay?" His voice turned bitter. "Are you with your lover?" He sighed. "Just let me know you're okay and I'll hang up."

I sighed. Kyle was being clingier than normal. "It's seven in the morning and I told you I needed my sleep. What's wrong with you? Of course I'm okay."

"You don't sound okay," Kyle said. "You sound like you've been crying."

Crap. I should be furious with Kyle – he knew that – but I was so heartbroken by what had happened with Danny that I couldn't bring myself to be mad. Before I could stop myself I blurted it out. "We broke up, okay?"

"So your casual and meaningless relationship...not so casual, huh?" Kyle was straining on the other end of the line.

"It was..." I started, before stopping myself. I didn't need to bitch to Kyle about my problems; in fact, that was absolutely the last thing I should do right now. "Oh, Kyle, I'm just being stupid. It's fine. I don't..."

"Where are you, Neve?" Kyle's voice was urgent. "I'll be right over."

"Kyle, it's okay."

"Neve – I'm sorry," Kyle said. "I've been a real jerk to you. But if you need me as a friend – *just* a friend – I am there for you, okay? I love you as a friend. Always have, always will. And if you don't have a best girlfriend – well, I can try to fill that role for you."

"Oh, Kyle..." He meant so well, I knew that. But he *couldn't* be my "best girlfriend" - not after the fight we'd had.

Before I could say anything, the door to my room flew open.

To anyone else, the sight of Keith Knight in a fuzzy white bathrobe, holding a baseball bat next to the negligee-clad figure of Jessica Botano, holding a fire extinguisher, would be something out of an LSD-induced hallucination. But to me, it was just Mom and Dad.

"I told you it was Never!" Mom turned to my father. "But you wouldn't listen. Put away your bat." She turned to me apologetically. "He thought it was burglars."

"Babe Ruth himself signed this bat, I'll have you know! And what are you doing back here, anyway?" My dad grinned. "You need to warn us first – your mom and I thought that once you were out of the house we could finally...have some fun."

"Keith!"

"Dad!" *Great.* Keith Knight, famous for the threesome he'd had with Mick and Bianca Jagger, was better at having a happy monogamous relationship than I was.

"Is that your parents?" Kyle's voice sounded urgent. "Are you at home? I'll be right over."

"Please don't," I said, as firmly as I could. "Do me a favor, Kyle. Go to bed. Be well-rested. That's the best thing you could do for the band right now – or for me."

"Sure," Kyle said, sounding disappointed. "Goodnight, Neve."

"Goodnight."

"So what are you doing back here, baby?" My mother sat down next to me on the bed.

I looked at my dad. "Guy stuff," I muttered.

"Out!" My mother declared, and my dad sighed and shuffled away. "Our daughter needs her Mommy, don't you, sweetie?"

"Goodnight, Crabcakes," my father said. "I can see where I'm not needed. Just tell me where to send the hit men."

"Dad!"

"I'm just saying – I know people."

"Is it Luc?" My mother hugged me.

"No."

"Kyle?"

"*Definitely* not!"

"Really," my mother looked perplexed. "I was sure it would be one or the other eventually."

"It's neither."

"Neither!"

"He's someone from school."

"Oh."

"We were together – and now we're...well, I guess we're broken up."

"You guess?"

"I kind of left before he could finish the job."

My mother hugged me close. "Oh, baby... sometimes things like that just happen, you know? Sometimes it's for the best. But even a bad relationship can teach you something important about yourself. Or what you want. It's a learning experience – even the painful ones. Especially the painful ones." I felt the tears well up in my eyes involuntarily. I couldn't help but think of Danny – how much I'd cared for him, how much I'd started to love him...

"I dated a lot of toads before I met your father," said my mother. "In the LA celebrity scene at that time – there were a *lot* of guys who weren't great to women. Guys who just wanted sex, guys who wanted total emotional control, guys who wanted you to give them cred in the tabloids – all of it. And your father wasn't such a peach when we met, either. He wasn't ready to settle down – be a family man. And for our first few years...it was hard..." she sighed. "We came pretty close to calling it quits a few times. And then we had you...and....well, it was a combination of things. Keith and I were both getting older, more mature. We'd been through so much together. And when you were born, your tiny fingers and teeny toes seemed so much more important than LA parties or the covers to tabloids...and now, your father and I couldn't be happier."

"Thanks, Mom," I snuggled into her arms, feeling like a child again.

"Whatever and whenever you need me," she said. "I can help you. But I can't help you unless you help yourself. Get some sleep before you do anything. You'll need to be fighting fit for your performance at the Palladium tomorrow."

My stomach dropped. "You know about that?"

"Of course I know," my mother said. "I listen to college radio. I've known for ages. I never said anything since I knew you wanted to keep it from your father – but...I'm proud of you."

"And Dad?"

"He wants to talk to you in the morning. But for now – sleep!"

*****

Things felt a little bit better in the morning – being in my childhood home, the familiar light streaming through the windows, made things seem a bit better. And then I remembered. Dad wanted to talk to me. I gritted my teeth as I changed into my pajamas. I knew how this conversation was going to go – I knew what Dad was going to tell me. To quit the band, to give it up. He was going to tell me the same lecture I'd heard so many times: that rock bands were no place for a teenage girl even at eighteen, that the scene was filled with sex, drugs, and booze, that he'd seen his friends die, choking on their own vomit, overdosing, dying of AIDS contracted from drug use or unsafe sex. He couldn't look at me – he'd said this many times before – without looking at his past, at his mistakes, mistakes that almost cost him his life, and with it the family he had today. I sighed. I wasn't in the mood to have this sort of conversation today, not after the day I'd had. Between my fight with Kyle and losing Danny, it was all I could do to get out of bed and shuffle into my slippers. I tried to dry my tears, to strengthen myself for the day. Whatever my dad said, whatever he threatened me with, I had to get to the Palladium tonight. I had to face Danny – even when seeing him made my heart break into a million little pieces. I had to face everything. I'd promised myself when I first started seeing Danny – I wouldn't let my drama interfere with the life of the band. I wouldn't let my heart get in the way of my voice. And that meant forcing myself to get through this day.

I walked into the dining room, where my father was already sitting in a black satin dressing gown, eating a plateful of eggs. He didn't look angry, I noted with surprise as I tentatively sat down next to him. His eyes were wide – almost sad – he sighed softly when I took the plate next to his and started to eat.

"Hey, Crabcakes."

"Hey, dad."

"Pretty rough week, huh?"

"You saw the post?"

"Who was that guy? The one who kissed you."

"A stalker called John Flint."

"Anyone you know?"

I shook my head.

"I had crazed fans too. Stalkers. One girl kept sending naked pictures of herself to the house, writing threatening letters to your mother. There are so many reasons to worry in this business – that was only one of them. The tabloid coverage – the constant supervision. I remember once, when your mother and I were first married...it was hard at first, Neve. I didn't give up being a rock star right away. I...saw other women. I was too drunk or too high to care that what I was doing hurt your mother. And then I saw that the tabloids had caught me with one of these women...and I knew your mother would see the pictures when she was checking out at the grocery store. And I knew then – at that moment – that if I wanted to keep a wonderful, smart, kind woman like your mother, I'd have to shape up. The life I'd lived as a rock star – it wasn't just the sex, Neve. Or the drugs. Or the lifestyle. It was the person I'd become: a person so strung-out and selfish that I couldn't see that I was about to lose the people I loved most. And that's what I don't want for you, Neve."

"Dad, it's not like that."

"When I saw that picture of you on TMZ, it was like seeing that picture of myself with...that woman all over again. A reminder of the life I used to lead. A reminder of the life I *cannot* lead if I want to be a good dad to you and a good husband to your mother. It's so easy, as a rock star, to get so wrapped up in your own drama and your own issues that you stop caring about the people around you."

I thought miserably of Danny.

"Then I decided to listen to you play. I listened to the single that your band put up on Myspace. Figured I'd have a listen before I judged. And it was *good*, Neve. Really good."

I blushed slightly. Dad had never complimented my music before. After all – how could any music I created measure up to the sounds of Keith Knight and his band?

"It reminded me of why I went into rock and roll to begin with. Not to get rich or famous. Not to get women or score drugs or get free booze. But to tell stories – beautiful stories – with music and with words. To touch people. To make them feel something." He looked up at me. "Your songs made me feel something, Never. Pride – in having a daughter so talented, able to find her own voice. I saw in the liner notes that you wrote some of the songs, Never. You have...something special. And you did it without me." He smiled. "And I'm proud of that too – as sad as it makes me to see my girl growing up. I was so afraid you'd turn into one of the other celebrity daughters I know – trying to make a career on the back of an over-indulgent father. *But* you weren't like that. You did it by yourself. And I've never been prouder of you than I am now, Never."

I was speechless – utterly shocked. After all this time I spent worrying about my father forbidding me to be in a band, was he giving me his blessing?

"This isn't an unqualified showing of support, Never," my dad continued, putting his hand on my knee. "I'm still worried about you. The lifestyle – the rock n' roll scene – it's no more innocent now than it was in the '70's and '80's. Maybe worse. And I worry about you – as my daughter, as a human being – of the way that fame can change you. There are so many dangers for a young woman these days. STDs, pregnancy, drug addiction – and don't think I'm being alarmist, Never; I've seen all these things happen to friends of mine back in the day." He looked up at me. "If you're going to do this, Never, at least let me keep you safe. Introduce you to the right people, the people you can trust. People who won't betray you or steal your money or try to get you hooked on drugs."

"I don't want you to interfere, Dad," I said, my voice choked with emotion. "I just want to make it on my own – every step of the way. I don't want to be just Keith Knight's daughter."

"But you'll always be my daughter, sweetheart," he said. "And I'll always love you." He hugged me tight. "You wow them tonight at the Palladium, okay?"

Tears were streaming down my cheeks. "Okay," I said.

There wasn't time to reflect on my conversation with my father. No sooner had we said our goodbyes than I had to hop into the shower and get ready for tonight. My father's strength had given me renewed energy, renewed vigor – the conviction that I had to *wow them* all tonight. Not just the audience, but Danny too. *Let him see what he's missing*, I thought angrily as I looked through my wardrobe, in search of the perfect outfit to show Danny precisely what he could have had – and what he'd lost. I decided to go all out – a deep black leather miniskirt with red trim, a lacy black bustier top that pushed up my breasts and emphasized their shape, and red faux-crocodile heels that added a few inches to my already not inconsiderable height. I left my hair long, allowing the dark tresses to flow freely around my face, lining my eyes with copious amounts of eyeliner to bring out the green-hazel tint Danny had once found so inviting...

"Damn..." Luc's mouth almost dropped open when he saw me. "I see you've dressed up for the occasion." His words were innocent, but his gaze was filled with desire – as was Kyle's. They'd never looked at me like that before – their eyes so strongly hinting at unbridled longing. Now that they knew I was dating around – now that they'd pictured me having meaningless sex with my mystery groupie – I couldn't be the asexual "kid sister" anymore, the girl they'd kidded themselves into thinking would never date, would never have any life outside the band. I flushed. Nothing was innocent anymore; it felt like my experience with Danny had colored all parts of my life.

You're just projecting, Neve, I tried to tell myself. *Stop worrying.*

Danny, by contrast, looked infinitely less well-rested. He wasn't wearing his customary leather and eyeliner. He was wearing tight jeans, his T-shirt casual and looking like he'd picked it crumpled off the floor. His stubble and the dark circles under his eyes betrayed the fact that he hadn't slept. The sight of him still sent my heart into a whirlwind of agony.

"Neve..." Danny came up to me, his eyes filled with pain.

"Glad to see you showed up." I was cool, calm, collected. I wasn't going to let him see how much his words had hurt me.

"Of course I did," Danny said. "I'd never let you or the band down. Neve, we need to talk. Can we..."

"There's nothing to say." I didn't want to deal with this right now. I had to focus on getting ready for the gig – I couldn't let myself give into the maelstrom of emotions inside me right now.

"There's a whole lot to say!" Danny insisted. "I've been trying to call you all day. And send emails. You haven't answered my calls, my messages, my texts." I'd turned off the phone after the first one – unwilling to deal with what I knew would be insincere apologies at best. Danny Blue didn't want a relationship with me, and that's all there was to it.

"Look, Danny," I said. "I *did* want something more, okay? I didn't just want sex – and I'm sorry. You want fun; I want a relationship. Let's be grown-ups and end it before we get hurt, okay?"

"Neve, I really want to talk about this."

"The show's going to start any minute, Danny..."

I passed him and went backstage, focusing on the lyrics, trying to remember them as I warmed up my voice, hoping I wouldn't cry...

I had to focus on the music – I had to let my mind go black, let the music flood through me, sublimating all my fears, all my pain. I had to let go of Danny, of my heart, of my pain, of everything but the song that flowed through me...

And we sang together. The music played. And once more we were beautiful, powerful, brilliant – once more we had the audience in the palm of our hands. I channeled my anger, my pain, my loneliness, all my feelings into the long loud wail of my voice.

I could feel the energy. It was electric. Through my pain, we'd managed to give our best performance yet.

Chapter 19

After the performance we were all utterly exhausted. I felt drained – the force and passion of my performance had left me completely spent. As we headed backstage – I was careful to avoid Danny's gaze – I couldn't help but feel completely overwhelmed by the past few weeks. In a matter of barely a month, I had watched the Never Knights go from a tiny indie band to the wildly successful opening act for the Cure. I had watched as the Never Knights – a close, tight-knight group of best friends – had slowly begun to unravel: first we'd lost Geoff, then gained Danny. Luc and Kyle were still tense around each other; Kyle and I had a lot to sort out, I knew. I'd fallen in love. I'd lost my virginity to Danny Blue, whose voice onstage and off still had the power to make me melt. I'd finally gotten the approval from my father that I'd been seeking for so long. Had it really been only this September that I'd arrived on the USC campus, a fresh-faced eighteen-year-old hoping to blend in, hoping to after eighteen years of privilege, start at last something resembling a normal life? That seemed like so long ago now. Standing onstage, hearing the raucous applause of thousands of people, listening to the echoes of the guitar and the drums reverberating through the whole amphitheater, I wondered if I would ever feel normal again. My fingers were calloused from the guitar I'd played; my voice was rough and ragged. I stumbled backstage and doused my face with cold water, trying to regain some sense of balance.

"Neve!" Danny came over to me. "Neve – you were incredible tonight."

"Thanks..." No sooner had he come near me than I was walking away, heading towards the reception area. "You too." I would not look at him, I told myself. I would not let him hurt me once more – would not give him the power of looking into my eyes and being able to tell precisely how much he had hurt me. He'd done enough – that final satisfaction of knowing the power he had over me was one I would never give him. Of course, he had seen me in my vulnerable moments. He had heard me cry out things, words I'd never thought I would cry out. He had seen my face and body unguarded as I lay back on the bed, writhing with pleasure, letting him know exactly the power he had over my body.

"Neve, I really want to talk to you. Look, about what happened the other night..."

"I don't want to discuss it," I said shortly as we walked into the reception room together.

"Neve!" A short, red-haired girl rushed up to me. She couldn't have been more than sixteen, but her goth makeup and mohawk suggested that she'd done a lot to try to look older. "Neve Knight – is it really you?"

"Yes?" I turned around, confused. "I'm sorry, do I know..."

"I'myourbiggestfan," she exclaimed – all in one single breath. "I mean, I'm sure you have others, but I'm the president of your official fan club."

"We have an official fan club?"

"Ever since last summer, when 'The Night is Young' hit college radio – I downloaded it and listened to it hundreds of times since then. It helped me through a lot – when I was dealing with this breakup I just listened to it on repeat and cried and cried. And I started the fan club. We come to all your shows. And this one was the best one yet!" She blushed, her face radiant with happiness. "I have all your EPs – and a couple of bootlegs. I mean – you're my heroine."

"Me?" I was flabbergasted. I knew that we were starting to make it big – that we were perched on the cusp of success – but I had never imagined that we'd have anything like a fan club yet. To my mind we were still that same idealistic group of kids who practiced in Luc's mom's basement three nights a week during high school.

"I mean – there's a lot of rock groups out there fronted by a girl. I know – I listen to a lot of music. But you're not just "the girl," you know. You don't just sing and look hot or whatever. You play guitar, too. And you write all your own songs. And you're totally cool just being one of the guys – I think that's so great." She smiled. "I'm starting a band now – with a few friends from the fan club. We learned to play 'The Night is Young' - we played it for my high school dance." Her face fell. "That's not like a copyright issue or anything, is it?"

"Don't worry about it." I smiled back at her.

I looked out through the corner of my eye. Danny had vanished into the crowd – I was surrounded by fans, groupies. People who not only cared about my appearance, but about my music. *Our music.* My heart was beating so loudly I could feel it in my ears; I'd never been so overjoyed in my life. For a moment, Danny didn't matter. Kyle didn't matter. The pain in my chest didn't matter. All I could feel was the overwhelming joy of having *succeeded* at last – the way I'd always wanted to. My music had touched somebody.

That was something not even Danny Blue could take away.

****

The next few weeks passed by in something of a blur. Our success at the Palladium had invigorated our internet sales, not to mention the press interest in us. Our booker called us the moment we left the Palladium – telling us that she'd, on the live-tweeted feedback alone, been able to book us another, smaller gig, for the next night and the next. Suddenly we'd gone from playing a show a month, if that, to playing a show every night or two for the next two weeks. I hardly had time to concentrate on my heartbreak. I spent all the time I had with the band practicing; those few moments that I had to spare I spent catching up on homework and trying desperately to get through midterms. But nothing was as difficult as sitting in Professor Poe's class, trying to present a paper on the glam rock movement. Whenever I walked into that classroom I could feel Danny's eyes on me, his stare boring through me. He wanted me – I could feel the force of his desire for me even when I turned away. But I knew now that all he wanted, all I could give him, was sex. And what I felt for Danny was so much more than that. While my desire for him had only increased in our separation, I knew now that I didn't want to fall back into the trap of becoming friends-with-benefits alone. As much as those nights gave me pleasure, I needed something more from him. Something that I knew he couldn't give.

Meanwhile, my relationship with Kyle started to stabilize somewhat. Since our semi-fight over my mysterious lover, Kyle had begun to chill out considerably. He was aware – all too aware – that he'd gone too far and said too much, and he worked extra hard to try and make us both forget the truth that had now come between us – the love he felt for me. "I just...got a little freaked out," he admitted as we walked between classes one day. "I'm so used to losing the people I love. I feel like I get attached to someone – and they go away. You were the only person in my life for so long, other than my aunt, who gave me stability. Who made me feel loved. I guess I got jealous – scared I'd lose you, lose that connection." He smiled. "But whatever happens – you're your own person, and you've got to make your own decisions. I get that." Still, as hard as he tried to whitewash what had happened, I could still see the naked, unbridled desire in his eyes. The look that made it clear that he wanted to do with me precisely what Danny had done.

We'd taken to practicing in the daytime at Luc and Kyle's, since we were at gigs all night – which made it possible to avoid the noise restrictions within reason. I was relieved. I wasn't sure how I would be able to handle going back to that cottage by the sea, looking at the bed that had been the source of so much pleasure, looking at the couch, the shower...all objects filled with lasting memories. If we went back there, I knew, it would take every inch of my concentration not to break down and sob. I tried to repress my feelings, to focus on the positive: the band was a success, and we were playing to packed houses every night. But somehow I couldn't feel as happy as I wanted to feel. Danny's absence was a dull ache in my heart.

And when our booker called to let me know that Beyond Blue, the Vegas outlet of Danny's family's chain hotel empire, had specifically requested that we play on their main stage, I was torn between excitement and disappointment. On the one hand, it was our highest-profile gig yet – a chance to travel to another city, to play to hundreds if not thousands of people. On the other hand – it was Danny's father's club. And that meant being closer to Danny, dealing with his family, dealing with a world to which I had gotten so close. If I had been Danny's girlfriend, I couldn't help but wonder bitterly, then would I have been introduced to his father? Would I have gone with him on those hotel trips like he promised?

If...

The word that stood between me and so much happiness.

Still, if my heartbreak was making me feel like my life was falling apart, it had the opposite effect on my music. I'd never played or sang better than I did that night at Beyond Blue. My heart was breaking every second I was onstage; just looking at Danny made me want to sob aloud, and tears sprang to my eyes as I looked into his own. But that pain, that anger – all that came out in a voice that barely seemed as if it were coming from me at all: it was a voice that was raw with emotion, a voice that conveyed so much, melding with the guitar solos to create a wall of sound, an overwhelming echolalia of expression. And the crowd was going wild for it.

Then came the last song – the song we'd practiced a hundred times before. My duet with Danny – a song that we'd written together the week he'd first joined the band. A song called "Don't Tell Me Why" about lost love. We'd composed it without thinking of its meaning – but now, singing it as we stared into each other's eyes, the words came to us as if for the first time. Danny and I – singing together:

"Don't tell me why it didn't work/don't tell me why it all went wrong," I began, and he continued where I left off.

"Don't tell me why I never knew/you were running all along."

"Don't tell me why you went away/don't tell me why you never stay...."

And then we looked at each other as we sang together: our voices melding together, his gaze so intense upon my own:

"Just tell me that you're coming home to me."

As we looked into one another's eyes, as I felt the piercing stare of his icy blue gaze, I couldn't help but feel a connection with him. Even now, even apart, I felt close to him: as if the music gave us a space, out of life, out of space and time, to be together. To be in love – even when I knew that love was impossible. My whole body ached for him – but something else ached too. My heart was broken. I felt it now more keenly than before.

"Just tell me that you're coming home."

Tears were streaming down my face as we packed up our instruments and headed backstage.

"You okay, Neve?" Steve came up to me.

"Just an intense show, that's all," I said, deflecting his question.

To our surprise, we found backstage for us a whole table piled high with gifts – presents from fans. A teddy bear, a few bouquets of red roses, chocolates, poems. One woman slyly slid me an envelope. I opened it, my mouth dropping open as I saw a series of black-and-white photographs of the woman fully unclad.

"I've got such a crush..." she began, blushing.

"You want me to give these to someone?" I asked. "Kyle...? Luc? *Danny?*"

The woman laughed. "Honey – they're for *you*. My number's written on the back."

Before I could respond, she winked at me and vanished. I stood holding the photographs in utter shock. So this was what being a rock star was like.

The manager tapped me lightly on the shoulder. "Miss Knight?" he said.

"Yes?"

"We've got a bit of a situation I was hoping you could help us resolve if you don't mind."

"Sure," I said, following him through a gorgeous corridor lined with marble and gilded mirrors, chandeliers hanging from the ceiling.

"Secret VIP entrance," said the manager, opening a hidden door in the wall and taking me into an elevator. "We're going all the way to the penthouse suite."

The penthouse suite? Had my mother and father decided to come see the show?

The manager smiled at me as we stood outside the door. "I think you'll find what you're looking for in there," he said. "And thanks for the show, Miss Knight. It meant a lot to me to be able to be there to see it."

I tentatively opened the door, gasping as I did so. The suite was the most beautiful room I'd ever seen. Luxurious, with a roaring fire in the fireplace and an elaborate four-poster bed piled high with satin curtains, this suite was more than just a VIP suite. It was the ultimate in luxury.

"Hello?" I called out, walking into the living room. Upon the table I spotted a bottle of champagne chilling in an ice bucket, lying next to a box of chocolates and a bowl of fresh, sweet-looking strawberries. Next to them was a note – unsigned:

"Just tell me that you're coming home to me."

My heart began to beat faster. "Hello?" I called out.

And then I heard it. A slow, sad melody from the bedroom – being strummed not on an electric guitar but rather on the melancholy strings of an acoustic. I walked in to find Danny sitting on the bed, dressed in black, looking up at me with soft, sweet eyes, smiling as he played.

"I know so many things/there's so much that I can do
"I can play the perfect fool/I can manage losing you"

His eyes filled with pain as he sang.

"I know how to play guitar/I know how to write a melody

I know how to make the girl I love fall out of love with me.

I've been holding on to too many ghosts/they hold me back I see

But no-one holds me back the way I do it all to me."

When the song was done, he put down his guitar and stood up, coming towards me. "I wrote it for you, Neve. It's the first romantic song I've written for anyone since Peyton died." He took my face in his hands, gently kissing me. "I was so stupid. I was so blind. What we had – it was more than just sex. You knew it. I knew it. But I freaked out, Neve. I thought that if I just focused on the sex, on the passion – I could protect my heart. I could stop myself from falling in love, from getting hurt again. But now I see just the opposite. I managed to hurt myself – and you – by being such a fool." He kissed me passionately, deeply. "And watching you sing these past few weeks – watching your talent grow every day. You have so much inside of you, Neve. So much passion. So much complexity. And you keep it bottled up. And when you let it out – either in your music or...in bed. It's beautiful, Neve. It's absolutely beautiful." He sat me down with him on the bed. "Since Peyton died, it's been so hard. I've had to deal with so much. The pain – the nightmares – the guilt. And only with you did that pain go away."

"I'm not a band-aid, Danny," I said softy. His words had moved me, but I was still scared. I knew he had the power to hurt me again – a power I didn't want to cede to him. "I can't just fix your problems, stop your pain."

"No, Neve," said Danny. "You are so much more than that to me. I feel like when I'm with you I understand you, and you understand me. I feel closer to you than to anyone in a long while. It was one thing if it was just the sex. But it's more than that. It's the energy that passes between us – this feeling that, when we're together, we're both so overwhelmed by happiness, by those feelings. When I met you, I admit it; it was attraction, plain and simple. But it's become so much more than that. These past few weeks I missed you so much. All I wanted to do was turn around, leave Chicago or New York, go home and rush into your arms right away. This is the first time I've felt like that, Neve. For a long time. Maybe ever."

I felt tears coming to my eyes again. This was everything I'd wanted to hear for so long, everything I'd wanted from Danny – overwhelming me all at once with its beauty. But I couldn't go back to him – not even now. Not unless I was sure he wouldn't hurt me like that again.

"I want to believe that, Danny," I said. "But I don't want just sex anymore. I want a relationship with you – a real one. It's that or nothing for me."

Before he could respond my phone vibrated. It was a text from Kyle. The rest of the band had gone out for drinks, and he was wondering where I was.

I called him back.

"Where are you?" he said. "We're about to drink to our success."

"The manager took me to a special suite. A fan wanted to give me a gift." I flushed. After all I had said about wanting a relationship with Danny, I knew that even if we had one, it could never be normal. We'd always have to keep it a secret.

"Oh," said Kyle. "Well, welcome to the perks of rock-star-dom I guess."

"I'll be busy," I said firmly. "Don't wait up for me."

As soon as I had hung up, Danny's mouth was on mine, his hands seeking the ribbon to my bustier. He was kissing me, overwhelming me with his caresses, feeling my breasts, the heat of my body, its warmth, driving me crazy.

"So, Kyle, huh?" he teased. "You want to make me jealous?" He laughed and kissed me. "I know he's spending a lot of time with you, lately." His lips brushed my nipple and made me shudder. "But I don't want him touching you. I don't want you with anyone – except me."

"Then I don't want *you* with anyone, except me. Danny..." My voice was husky with need.

"I want you, Nev," he said. "Take me back – please say you'll take me back."

"Only if it's real, Danny. If it's more than sex."

"I said it in my song, Neve. I need you."

"If you need me..." I pulled up my bustier, putting my shoes back on. "Then meet me halfway, Danny."

He said nothing and I sighed. My heart sank again. All these words meant nothing, I knew, without commitment. "Look, Kyle and the guys are downstairs – I should probably..."

"Neve, wait!" Danny called after me. "Don't leave me, please." He sounded so vulnerable all of a sudden. Lost. Confused. "Please don't go..." His eyes were wide with pain – his face was hollow, almost empty. Tears were in his eyes. "I can't go back to it. To life before you. To the nightmares."

I relented. "Don't worry," I said. "I'm not going anywhere. But you need to talk to me. To explain." I kissed his forehead. "Let me know what you're thinking."

He relaxed in my arms, but I could still sense his pain. "You really want to know?"

"I do," I said. "If we're going to have a relationship – we need to be honest with each other, open."

Danny looked up into my eyes, his gaze full of tears. "So you'll stay."

"If you tell me what's going on. If you open up."

Danny rose and went to his guitar, holding it against him like a safety blanket. We sat for a while in silence. At last he spoke.

Chapter 20

"Peyton," Danny began. "I used to think she was the only girl in the world who understood me. Understood what it was like to grow up the way I did. Always in the shadow of my dad. No matter what I did, I'd never be as clever, as attractive, as rich, as interesting as the famous Clarence Blue. Everyone loved him. Or at least – everyone wanted favors from him. And he gave me plenty. Summers in Switzerland. Winters in Majorca. A Fender strat at the age of five. Everything, that is, but attention. But love. He was so busy, so wrapped up in being Clarence Blue, in being popular and loved and famous, that he forgot he had a son. Having a son would be bad for his image, you see. After all, Clarence Blue is an international playboy, not a doting dad."

I thought of my own father – so willing to give up his rock star days for his family – and felt lucky.

"You don't know what it's like growing up with a different stepmother every year. Some of them barely older than me. All of them so lonely, so unhappy. They'd married my father because they were in love with his image – only to find that he'd ignore them, neglect them, cheat on them in turn. He didn't care about them. Some of them turned to me, tried to seduce me in order to get revenge on my dad for cheating on them – but I never did. I just wanted to get away, to get out. To be free of my whole family and its crazy dysfunction. And my world really was crazy, insane. Sometimes I wonder if my dad really is stark raving mad. All he cares about is power – and this obsession with power consumed him. He married my mother before he was wealthy – he was a young upstart; she was a fashion model who worked at his company to pay the bills. She died when I was ten. Car accident. Since then...he made his billions and decided to *buy* women instead of falling in love with them. He just wanted to be seen with a different woman on his arm at every function – he didn't care about his family. But when I met Peyton...things were different. I was just eighteen and she was older, twenty-one. I had just come up to Oxford to study music and she was in her final year. Everyone knew she'd get the highest first-class degree in the year – her talent was extraordinary. She studied classical voice and piano, but what she really wanted to do was make music. Real, gritty English punk – like Joy Division or the Clash. Not the sort of thing you expect in a posh place like Oxford. She was from a normal, middle-class family from Chester. A warm, loving family. They gave me attention, kindness, everything I lacked. I even spent Christmas with them. And she taught me a lot about being a musician. And a lot about making love. She was more experienced than I was by far, but she was a kind and patient teacher. She taught me how wonderful it could be to make someone you love happy in that way. She helped me overcome my insecurities; she gave me so much confidence. She encouraged me to pursue what I wanted instead of what my father wanted for me; she inspired me to apply to the doctoral program at USC, to complement my love of playing music with my academic interest in it." He paused. "I'm sorry, Neve. I know it must be hard for you, hearing me talk about her. But you wanted to know everything..."

It was. But feeling Danny open up before me – I felt that for the first time we were really getting somewhere, getting closer. "Go on," I said.

"Last year we were driving back from a gig in Manchester, where I was on summer holiday. I was absolutely exhausted – completely shattered, overworked. I hadn't been drinking that night, but I'd been taking energy pills – caffeine pills, Adderall, anything legal or illegal to give me energy. I was trying to do so much at once – be a good boyfriend, do my doctoral work, play in the band, that I started abusing uppers. And I was so completely exhausted – but I insisted on driving anyway. She said I was tired, to let her drive instead, but I refused. I was arrogant. I wanted to prove to her that I was strong. That I could do it all. That I could handle the stress – no matter what my father thought. And I handled it, all right. Crashed from the high, fell asleep at the wheel, drove into a tree at eighty miles an hour. Of course, I escaped without a scratch. Fate's funny that way. But Peyton..." He began to sob. "Neve, when I woke up, she was dead right in front of me. She was killed instantly."

I took him in my arms, wanting to soothe him, to take away his pain. "If I'd listened to her, if I hadn't been so bloody arrogant – she'd still be alive, Neve. But I wanted to prove to her – my blasted male ego! - prove to her that I had the strength and capacity to do it all. And I got the woman I loved, killed. I killed Peyton, and I'll have to live with that guilt for the rest of my life."

His lips trembled, and I wanted nothing more than to stop the pain, to sooth him, to dry his tears. I leaned in to kiss him, but he turned away.

"How can you love me?" he asked, his voice raspy, his face streaming with tears. "When I can't even stand to look at myself in the mirror. How can you want to be with me – when I've killed the only woman I loved?"

"Because I know you," I found myself crying. I was kissing away his tears, tasting the salt, tasting the salt that came from my own tears that had begun to flow and mingle with his. "Because I trust you. I know who you are. You're a good person. And I do care for you – because you deserve someone who does."

Before I knew it I was unbuttoning his shirt, pulling down his trousers, covering his body with my own, communicating how much I cared for him in the only way he can accept my love... through sex. The sex was not passionate that night – not in the sense that it had been – raging, hormonal, all-consuming. But it was something else. It was intimate, warm, loving. Even romantic. Our lips touched the whole time – as our bodies merged, we rejoiced in giving one another pleasure, rejoiced in being so close together, in holding one another, in letting out all our pain, all our secrets. In crying together – intimate, at last.

That night I fell asleep in his arms. That night he slept soundly – his face beatific in slumber. That night, I knew, there would be no nightmares.

Chapter 21

Being back together with Danny was a glorious – even ecstatic – experience. The next morning, over breakfast, we cuddled naked and at last discussed what we were to each other. "Girlfriend" and "Boyfriend" - the terms sounded strange to us, at first, but deep down we both knew that they were the right ones. It would take time for both of us – for me to get over the hurt of Danny's initial reluctance, for him to get past his guilt and the shadow of Peyton that hung over us both. But for all that, I knew, we had something special; we would get through this together.

What we had, became more than just the sex – which, while still mind-blowing in its physical sensations, became increasingly soft, romantic, intimate, even gentle. We had a relationship at last. Some nights we curled up on the couch next to each other watching old movies and fell asleep, exhausted but happy. Some nights Danny drove me to a nearby town, or to a beach he knew – somewhere where we were in no danger of being recognized – and those were the best nights of all. When, far away from the band, far away from the fear of being discovered, we could hold hands in public and kiss and laugh like a normal couple.

Our dating, however, made our interactions in the places we knew more difficult to hide. In class, Danny had to force himself to avoid my gaze altogether, lest we both break into secret giggles during his lectures. During band practice, we constantly found ourselves looking into each other's eyes, staring at each other, transported by our rapture and by our desire for one another. We took every excuse to touch each other – handing each other instruments, helping each other carry bags or books – enjoying the secret electricity between us. Our newfound happiness made us almost careless; we both glowed with the radiance that came from being together.

Our performances only improved. Each night we were onstage, playing our hearts out – my joy sublimated into great music just as my pain had been. Our emotions gave the words of our songs new life. And every night, after the show, I would circle my car around the block a few times to throw the others off the scent before heading to Danny's ocean side cottage, before we threw ourselves into each other's arms and gave into the passion that had been building all evening.

It was one such morning – a few weeks into our relationship – that I had spent the night with Danny, enjoying a delirious night of unbridled sex followed by long conversations that kept us awake until dawn – that I had just stepped out of the shower, wrapping myself in one of Danny's old college sweatshirts from Oxford University, to keep warm. We'd ordered a late-night pizza that had, by now, turned into breakfast.

I heard a knock at the door. "Danny, is the pizza here?" I asked, stepping out of the bathroom, my hair still soaked. "Hurry up and let's get back to bed, because..."

I stopped short. Standing at the door was Kyle, his eyes wide with shock, a look of utter agony on his face. "I thought I left my keyboard plug here..." Kyle's voice was wobbling. "I guess I came at a bad time, huh." His face turned red then white again, his eyes dark as hurt, then anger, then fury spread across his face. I'd never seen so much pain in those angelic eyes of him; my heart ached for him. Still, I braced myself, knowing what was to come. If Kyle had been jealous of Luc, then that was nothing compared to this.

"Kyle..." I started, stuttering.

He was inhaling deeply, choking on his own air, rocking back and forth as he hyperventilated, trying to come to terms with the shock of the situation. "All this time," he said, his voice shaking. "All this time – you were with *him*! I can't believe it." He looked over at Danny. "And you....*you*! I thought you were my friend, my buddy. And you were screwing Neve this whole time! Behind our backs! I trusted you – *trusted you both*." Tears began to stream down his face. "It's true, isn't it? This time."

I couldn't lie to him. "Yes, it's true."

"But *him*!" Kyle sighed. "Why...why not me?"

My heart broke for him. I wanted to say something – anything – to make the pain stop, to make this better. But I knew that there was nothing I could do.

"Listen, mate..." Danny went over to Kyle. "I care about Neve and I'll treat her right, I promised. We wanted to keep our personal life separate from the..."

But he never got to finish his sentence. Kyle punched him square in the stomach, sending Danny reeling backwards across the room, crashing onto the floor.

"Listen, man – I'm sorry..." Danny was winded, breathless.

Kyle crossed the room swiftly, taking my hands in his. "You knew I loved you, Nev. I don't get it. You knew I loved you!"

It was all I could do to keep from sobbing. "I love you, Kyle. But not in that way. You know that. And nothing about me or Danny – nothing would have changed that. I don't feel that way about you....I've been honest about that."

"But you love Danny?"

I hesitated before I spoke. "Yes," I said, at last.

"Fine," Kyle spat. "Then you can have your band without me."

"Kyle – wait!"

But it was too late. He'd already stormed out and slammed the door behind him.

Epilogue

Calling Steve that afternoon was the hardest thing I'd had to do. I'd wanted to go after Kyle, to talk him down, to convince him to stay, but Danny convinced me that seeing me was the last thing Kyle wanted to do right now. "He needs some time to blow off steam," Danny said. "To rest." So I called Steve instead – figuring that he, as the only level-headed one in the band – not to mention the only one that wasn't trying to sleep with me – would know what to do.

To my relief, Steve didn't seem upset or angry. Instead, he laughed slightly. "I can't say I didn't guess," he said. "The chemistry was – pretty obvious. To me, at least. But the others – Kyle, especially… they didn't want to see it. But I guessed. When the two of you sang, it made *me* want to get a room." He teased me. "I guess you're not the flat-chested freckled kid anymore, are you Neve? Can you believe it? Guys want *you*?"

I laughed and teased back. "Don't look at me! How

does a scrawny gingerhead like you get so much female attention!"

But then Steve turned serious. "Look, Neve. I love you and all that – but not that way. Luckily. But I'm not sure how Luc's going to react to all this. He's a good friend of mine – we talk. And I know how he feels about you. I've always told Luc to make a move, to ask you out. But he held off – because he knew you'd never date anyone in the band..."

My heart sank. It was one thing to deal with just Kyle, but having to hurt Luc, too.

"I can talk to him if you want – but it's better if he hears it directly from you. Maybe it will hurt less that way."

"Steve, if there's anything you can do, can say, to make sure the band stays together."

"Maybe they will see reason," Steve said. "Maybe they won't. Luc might be able to pull it together, but I'm really not sure about Kyle. He's not exactly stable, is he..."

"No, not quite," I admitted. "He's been through a lot." I exhaled sharply.

"And both of them – in the same band, in the same room, as you and Danny – a constant reminder that he succeeded where they failed..."

"What do we do?"

"We'll have to give them time."

Time, unfortunately, wasn't something we had a lot of right now. No sooner had I said goodbye to Steve than I got another call – this time from Richard Slayton. The call I'd been waiting to get for weeks, months, years. The call that said that we'd proven ourselves at last, that at last we'd gotten a gig, that RRR wanted to sign us, produce our first album, take us on tour. Weeks ago the call would have elated me; I would have been overwhelmed with joy. Now I only felt numb. We had a record deal – but, as far as I knew, we didn't have a band.

I looked up at Danny, who was cradling me, his arms around my shoulders.

"What do we do?"

He sighed. "I don't know, Neve..." He forced himself to smile – a proud, loving smile – as he wrapped his arms around me. He kissed me passionately. "I'm so proud of you, Neve. You've wanted this forever. And I've wanted this for you." He pulled away. "I'm not going anywhere, Neve. I want this relationship to work. But I don't want to get in the way – band-wise."

"What are you saying?"

"Geoff's arm's almost healed by now. He'd be able to play instead of me. Maybe it'd be easier on the guys if you and I were dating – but I wasn't in the band. Maybe that's the way to play it."

"Danny, no...if we get this gig, we'll be traveling all the time. Going from city to city, going abroad. We'd be separated."

His eyes clouded. "I'll be around for you Neve. No matter what. But if I have to drop out of the band to hold onto you – and to keep your band together – then that's what we'll do." He kissed me, wrapping his arms around me. I sighed. Being apart from Danny would be torture, I knew. The music we made together inspired me, invigorated me.

But if Kyle and Luc couldn't handle me and Danny, this was the only way...

"What do you think, Neve?"

I nodded, slowly. "I don't know," I said. I shivered. Everything had changed so quickly – everything felt like it was spinning all around me.

Two months – and everything had changed. Two months...

My dream was coming true, and all I could think of

was losing Danny's arms around me, even for an instant. Losing the sight of him across the stage from me, his passion for me so clear on his face.

The band couldn't survive with him. But could it survive without him, either?

Never, Danny, Kyle, Luc, and Steve's story
continues in
Book 2 of the Never Knights Series

Never Land (Never Knights Series #2)

September 2012

Preview from the upcoming

Never Land

Volume 2 of the Never Knights Series

kailin gow

Prologue

London was burning. The sweat on my body and the lights that illuminated the club; the heat emanating from all of us in a single, nuclear force – all of these conspired to make the stage look like it was on fire. Steve's drums were deafening – powerful sticks hitting and throbbing against the center of the set, each clash echoing throughout the room. The guitar licks sent shivers up and down my body; I watched as the dancers moved and swayed and shouted in unison, singing along to our songs. Beautiful people – models, actors, wannabe writers, all falling under our spell. All charmed by our power.

> *"You said that you loved me/but I'm not sure*
> *I've been burned by you before."*

My voice hardly sounded like my own. Eerily echoing out of the microphone, it was louder than I was used to. Stronger. Filled with a magic that seemed to transform it from the voice of a nervous, eighteen-year-old girl into something far greater. A voice that could affect each and every one of these people, a voice that could get inside their heads and hearts and make them dance like their lives depended on it. The sweat was pouring down my body and I could catch a glimpse of sweat, too, on the faces of my bandmates, who were rapt in concentration, lost in the music. And I was lost, too – wandering through a labyrinth of sound, trying to find my way out of this energy, this power, this beautiful music that at once belonged to me and yet was something wholly other, some great mystery I had only just begun to learn how to unfold. The song was catchy – mesmerizing, even – but it was more than that. Its beauty haunted me – now more than ever. I had written the lyrics – they were part of me, etched on my heart.

But the music....

I hadn't written that alone. Some chord changes, some waverings of my voice – those I had come up with on my own. Those seemed familiar to me, even natural. But every now and then I changed key, or switched to a minor chord, or the sound of an A diminished wailed over the amplifiers – and then I remembered. Remembered that I hadn't written this song by myself. That another voice, another mind, was here in the room with me, even though he was so far away...

Danny...

My heart ached, even now. But I couldn't let myself think about that. Not when I had to put on a brave face in front of so many thousands – even tens of thousands – of people. Not when I had to convince them that I was more than just Keith Knight's protege daughter. I had to convince them that I was a rock star.

And from the wild sounds of their applause, it sounded like I was succeeding. When the song came to an end my voice was hoarse, husky. But even now it was filled with joy. Being onstage was exhilarating for me, for all of us. Only when I was singing did I truly feel as if I were home. And the audience picked up on that. They knew it as well as I did – that I was where I belonged, right here in the O2 arena, opening for My Bloody Valentine.

Six months ago we could never have dreamed this would happen. Six months ago, I was just starting college at USC, trying to fit in, trying to convince myself I wanted a normal life. But a lot had changed since then.

"Ladies and gentlemen," I began, my voice hardly wavering. "I give you – the Never Knights."

The crowd was riotous with joy. I recognized a few faces – celebrities I'd seen on the covers of British tabloids, aspiring reality stars and minor members of the Royal Family. But most of the crowd was full of strangers. A blessed relief, I thought, after LA – where the club scene was dominated by the same few faces, the same familiar smiles. Here everyone was new – the whole scene was wild, was different. Nobody knew us here; nobody had seen my pictures on TMZ or Gawker. They were willing to accept us on one thing along: the music.

"I'm Neve Knight, on vocals." The crowd responded almost immediately to me, a writhing mass of applause, of adoration. *You could get drunk on this*, I thought to myself, feeling myself bathed in the glow of their love. I felt dizzy just standing there before them. I was reeling – exhausted. And yet I wouldn't have given this up for anything in the world.

"And this is Steve Saint Clair, on drums..." I remembered how it had been only a few months ago, giving this same speech in a nightclub in Los Angeles. How much younger we had been then. Before the night everything changed. Before I'd met *him*. Shiny new stage name aside, Steve was still the same as ever. Gawky, charming, with an indomitably goofy smile that made girls giggle and swoon at the same time. He was the most solid of the lot of us – the only one who had come through the latest drama unscathed. Steve had never worried about anything but the band – he was the only one, for all his one-night stands, who never let his relationships come between him and the band. Something I knew I couldn't say for myself.

"And Lucky Luc, on keyboards." The girls went wild as Luc fixed his soulful chocolate-brown stare on the audience. *Lucky Luc, all right...*I thought. Our agent had picked the name – figured that a guy with killer looks like his had the luck of one in a million. But I knew that beneath Luc's movie-star good looks there lay a veneer of darkness, of sadness I was unable to crack. Luc hadn't been as violent as Kyle when he'd found out that Danny and I were dating. He hadn't threatened to leave the band overtly – as Kyle had done. But I'd seen the pain I caused in those deep brown eyes. I'd seen how hard it was for him to agree to stay, knowing that the girl he'd kissed in a moment of weakness, the girl he'd finally admitted his feelings to after so many years keeping it quiet, was in love with someone else. I couldn't talk to him about it, of course. We'd agreed to act like it never happened – to forget that kiss. But I knew that things weren't as they were between us. Whatever Luc felt for me, it hadn't gone away. And when he turned that classic, heart-melting stare upon me, it was getting even harder for me to catch my breath.

"And, on bass guitar, Kyle X." The other boys had changed their names for reasons of fame and fortune – because they wanted to re-invent themselves in the manner of their rock icons, taking on stage names that meant something to them. But in changing his name, I knew, Kyle Jostens was doing more than playing a part. He was running away from something. Running from the father whose name he bore, the father who had shot his mother, who was serving twenty to life in a federal penitentiary in California. But then again, Kyle was always running. From the pain – from the terror of abandonment, that had set in the day he lost the only family he'd ever known in a single, fell swoop. For years I'd been Kyle's family, his confidante. Like a sister to him.

But no more. He'd admitted his feelings for me – more than that, he'd let his desire for me get between the band. Threatened to walk out if Danny Blue stayed another day. I'd done what was necessary to make him stay – I'd apologized, cried, bitten down my pride and my anger and admitted I was wrong to fall for Danny Blue, even as my heart still told me I was right.

He'd agreed, in the end, to stay. Slowly, grudgingly. But he'd agreed nonetheless. But on one terrible condition.

"Geoff Galaxy, on guitars." It was hard even to form the words. Once upon a time, Geoff had been a true part of the band, one of our best friends. But for years now, drugs and alcohol had worked their way into Geoff's system, making him a mere shadow of the man he was. Geoff was still heart-breakingly beautiful; his shaved head and glinting earring still gave him the appearance of a dissolute pirate. And now that his hand had healed, he played guitar as well as he ever did. But something about him didn't sit right with me. It wasn't just the way he looked at me – smirking, predatory, as if he knew the real reason we invited him back into the band. It was the knowledge that cocaine and – no doubt – heroin had burned away some portion of humanity in his brain; the knowledge that the dangerous, devil-may-care persona he projected onstage was more than just an act.

Geoff was a ticking time bomb, and everybody knew it.

But in the absence of Danny Blue, he was the only chance we had. My heart sank as I remembered how Danny had once stood where Geoff was standing now, his smile genuine, his face unscarred by the ravages of drugs and drink. It had been a month since Danny had graciously stepped down from the band, knowing it was the only way to reconcile me and Kyle. And during that month I hadn't stopped missing him.

My heart skipped a beat as I remembered. *Tonight.* Tonight Danny's semester ended – his TA-ing gig at USC over for the semester. Tonight he was coming to London to celebrate Christmas and New Year's with me. I'd taken the year off to go touring – meaning that both of the obstacles between me and Danny had been removed in one fell swoop. He was no longer my band mate and no longer my TA.

That should have made things easy. Instead, we had an ocean between us. And hadn't seen each other in a month. Until tonight...

"Well done," a gorgeous black woman with long, curly hair and a killer smile approached us. She was

Cassandra Curry, the PR machine RRR had appointed for us shortly after signing us to their label. But she looked every inch the rock star. "A great start to your touring season. But the press is going to want photos. Look candid, okay guys?" She looked me up and down. "White leather dress," she assessed my clothing. "Vivienne Westwood?"

I nodded, stunned at the breadth of her knowledge.

"Not a bad choice," she smiled. "Shows off your skin. And the spikey boots are a nice touch, too. Although normally I avoid Cavalli's winter collections." She nodded. "I'll put them both on the label's tab. Fashion's part of marketing, after all."

She led us across a red carpet. The crowd passed over us in a blur – a whirl of screams, applause, autographs, blown kisses – and then we were safely backstage, digging into an enormous cake the venue had provided for us.

Kyle looked utterly exhausted. His bright blue eyes shone with joy – but I could see the melancholy within. Things hadn't been the same with us since our fight. He'd shown me a side of himself I'd never wanted to see – a crazed, obsessive darkness that I could forgive, but not forget. Kyle did more than love me – he *needed* me. And it was this need, a need I could never fulfill, that made things so terrible between us.

"Congratulations, Neve," he said in a small voice. "We've always dreamed about this, you know. Ever since we were kids. Performing in London. Birthplace of punk rock. And at the O2 arena, no less, opening for My Bloody Valentine..."

"I know!" *We'd made it.* We'd lived the dream. In that moment I wanted so badly for things to go back the way to they used to be, for Kyle and I to be normal with each other again. I couldn't resist it. I let my arms surround him, hugging him tightly, the way I'd done in the old days. *Wishing it could be the way it was in the old days.* I pressed his head to mine. "We did it."

I felt his body tense up. I felt his breathing grow shallow. No sooner did he turn his baby-blue eyes to mine than I knew it had been a mistake. Our faces were close – painfully close. And I knew then that I'd given him hope.

"Neve..." he said hoarsely, his voice ragged with emotion.

I immediately stepped away. "Kyle, I'm so sorry..." I said as quickly as I could. "Was that weird? I didn't mean to be weird..."

I couldn't give him hope. Not now. Not with Danny on his way to Heathrow as we spoke.

"No, I'm sorry..." Kyle looked down. "I've been a jerk, Neve, I know that. I knew that when I signed up for the band again. That you're with Danny now. I get that. I respect it. But that doesn't mean it's not still hard. I can't just turn off my feelings like a tap." He smiled wanly, trying hard to look nonchalant. "But for your sake. For the sake of the band. I have to try."

"I know, Kyle." I tried to give him a "buddy" pat on the shoulder. "We'll keep things professional from now on."

"As if that would help," he muttered under his breath. "I just need time, Neve. That's all. Time to get used to this."

I nodded. "I understand."

Steve interrupted our reverie, turning up with a girl on each arm. *Typical Steve,* I thought. Clearly he wasn't hung up on emotional drama. "These two want to come back to our suite," he smiled. "But I can't give them both the attention they deserve." He looked the girls up and down. "How about I bring along my friend Kyle here!"

Their enthusiastic moans made it clear what they thought of this proposal.

"So, Kyle can join us? Will you, Kyle?"

Kyle looked at me for a second, holding my gaze. I could feel his anguish, and even now it had the power to move me.

"Yeah, sure," Kyle said, moving away and following Steve.

No sooner had he gone than my phone rang. My heart leaped at the name on my caller ID: DANNY BLUE.

"Hello, love." His voice still had the power to galvanize me. "I've graded all the term papers – all twenty-five of them. And you know what that means?"

My body began to tingle.

"I've got nothing to do for the next leg of the flight except think about you. I'm sitting in Dublin airport right now, waiting for my connecting flight. If all goes well, I'll have you in my arms in a few short hours."

"Dublin, already?"

"Good winds," said Danny. "We got in early. Now I suggest you take a nap, love. Because you're not getting any sleep tonight."

His voice made me tremble with desire.

"Goodbye, love," he said.

"Goodbye – love you."

"See you soon."

My heart sank. He still hadn't said it back – those three little words I couldn't *stop* saying. I knew the history of his heart. Knew about the girl he had loved, whom he had accidentally killed – the girl I could never be. *Peyton.*

Had he said *I love you* to her?

I sighed and tried to ignore the prickling feelings of doubt. Danny and I were together, were happy. Why did I have to ruin it with my neuroses?

"So, Neve." A harsh, cold voice made me turn around. "I hear you got loads of action when I was away? I thought you were saving yourself, huh? But I guess you're just a dumb slut like all the rest."

My heart sank.

It was Geoff.

If you liked Never Say Never, you would like:

Aspiring psychiatrist Samantha Sullivan (Sam) never thought she would fall for the one mysterious guy she has been speaking to over the phone for months, the boy the counselors called Daggers. She wasn't supposed to talk to him outside of their sessions. But as she began to peel the layers of Daggers and learn who he is, the one boy she is supposed to be saving, might just be the one who is saving her. **YA-Mature/Older Teens/New Adults**

Want to Know More about *The Never Knights Series*, Author Insight, Author Appearance, Contests and Giveaways?

Join the Kailin Gow's Official Facebook Fan Page at:

http://www.facebook.com/KailinGowBooks

Talk to Kailin Gow, the bestselling author of over 100 distinct books for all ages at:

http://kailingow.wordpress.com

and

on Twitter at: @kailingow